Finding Adam
Empowering Susan

By

Rick Birk

ISBN no. 978-0-9819964-5-5

Library of Congress Categories: Psychology: Sensation.
Consciousness. Cognition. Parapsychology: Sleep.
Dreaming. Visions. Hypnotism. Phobias. Social phobias.
Agoraphobia. Past life regression. Suggestion. Subliminal
projection. Telepathy. Thought transference. Suffering.
Spiritualism. Reincarnation. Genealogy. Metaphysics.
Ontology. Philosophy.

This book is easily available at go5books.com

Author's Note

This narrative is based on factual information. A few names and events have been altered to protect privacy. To better serve the reader, this book is categorized as "Biographical Fiction." In choosing this classification, the author declares that *Finding Adam Empowering Susan* blends life experiences with fictional elements.

What people are saying about
Finding Adam Empowering Susan

"Past Life Regression is a way to unlock the door to the past. Rick Birk uses this tool in the case of Adam Evans, a conscientious man whose phobia seems to hinge on some bizarre event in his past. His journey inspires us to take stock of our own lives and self-awareness. It is all about coming together in life, in history and with the people in our lives."

-Dr. Virginia Ray Long, Certified (IBRT)
Past Life Regression Therapist, Scottsdale, AZ

"A tip of the hat to author Rick Birk, a descendant of Salem Witch Trials victim Susannah Martin, for not succumbing to the temptation to trivialize that terrible episode in American history for commercial purposes. Birk chooses instead to use the tragedy – and this, his latest book – as a vehicle for promoting tolerance, healing, forgiveness, and self-awareness."

-Jim McAllister, Historian and author, Salem, MA

"*Finding Adam Empowering Susan* is a compelling exploration into the three levels of our minds ... subconscious, conscious & super-conscious. In following Adam's quest, you will find yourself asking 'Could Adam's discoveries unlock parts of me that I don't understand?' This book may provide important keys to your own exciting discoveries."

-Sharon Crain, Ph.D. Educational Psychology, Scottsdale, AZ

What people are saying about
Finding Adam Empowering Susan

"I applaud Rick Birk's sensitive and respectful use of the Salem Witch Trials history and his connection to Susannah Martin in particular to explore views on agoraphobia, reincarnation, and faith. *Finding Adam Empowering Susan* is a fast-moving, interesting read."

-Alison D'Amario, Educational Director -
Salem Witch Museum, Salem, MA

"This is a moving story that reaches into the malignant memories buried in our souls, a labyrinth of hallways we may have never walked nor remembered. A terrifying tale of fear unleashed and of courage conquered. This author writes about a path anyone can choose when awakened, a story that has you picking through a mire of pain while seeking redemption and ultimately finding joy. Read this book and within the pages you may find yourself."

-Jennifer Ware, M.A. Education,
Psychiatric Clinical Case Manager, Phoenix, AZ

"*Finding Adam Empowering Susan* safely brings the reader face-to-face with the dark, often distressful realm of irrational fear but without suffering it's unfortunate consequences. Author Rick Birk entrances the reader's curiosity while at the same time teasing a compelling desire to confront our own self-doubts. *Finding Adam Empowering Susan* provides a unique perspective on how some fears are derived and potential coping options, but adds a novel twist. Some emotional afflictions are born not from present life circumstances but from our undiscovered past, quite possibly driven by Divine intent. The story charts a trail not commonly followed in real life and leads to an equally uncommon and exciting conclusion."

-Barry Marks, M.A. Education - School Psychology, Surprise, AZ

Acknowledgments

John Birk
Tom Birk
Hawthorne Hotel
Marilynne Roach
Ada Roberts
Donald Roberts
Tammy Townsend

Dedication

To all those who suffer from phobias yet have the strength to face the tempest, I applaud you. Each of you shows the courage to not only go forward in your desperate pursuit of hope and self-awareness but, more significantly, the nerve to encounter your demons.

Prologue

We are all human, capable of a multitude of accomplishments in our lives on earth. No two of us are the same. So what makes each of us unique? Most would say upbringing, heredity, traits, customs, environment, parents, genes, and perhaps human nature itself. Out of these emerge our beliefs, hopes, fears, mannerisms, dreams, and desires. All these in turn, mark how we respond to each and every bend along life's road. This is ... consciousness.

However, we must concede that all these variables are certainly not controllable. Moreover, are all potential factors even accounted for? Could it be possible there exists a certain unidentified, uncontrollable element of immense influence that compels us to maneuver through our days as we do? Could rudimentary memories imbedded deep in the core of our souls be the groundwork of our existence and accompany us life to life, and perhaps generation to generation? Might these emotional recollections be so monumental that all other factors pale in comparison?

More significantly, could these rudiments of memory, a gift from on high, allow us to uncover the truth of who we are and where we have been? Subsequently, might man's ultimate reward provided from this everlasting, timeless power of nature be the opportunity to live and to embrace our greatest stratum of existence?

Chapter One

As long as I can ever remember, I have always been different from most people. We all have our moments when we lack confidence in ourselves or our abilities. We feel that we don't measure up and deem ourselves less fortunate than others. After all, looks, IQ, athletic prowess, and charisma are so endeared by society that we are constantly in a comparison mode. But this is not entirely where I am coming from. I have always felt that, beyond any of these, I was in fact uncharacteristic.

To say that I marched to the beat of a different drummer seems a vast understatement. I saw, felt, heard, and understood life from an entirely outside perspective. My uniqueness and idiosyncrasies placed me front and center, showcased me on my very own life stage, as a production in no way destined to generate a sellout performance. I envisioned a magical cover enveloping my being that would not let me participate fully in life, and rendering me woefully introverted. Over the years, I grew to accept this part of me as if I were a child born with a missing limb. As an adolescent I spent great expanses of time alone, surviving in my own proverbial little world, similar to that of the ceaselessly shuffling long-distance runner.

I came into this world on July 19, 1985, in Portland, Oregon as Adam Michael Evans, the product of loving parents. I am the only child of Michael and Karen Evans. My older brother, Michael, Jr., had died within a few months of birth. This had always been an painful subject for both my parents. I once overheard Mom mention that Michael had been born with six toes on his right foot. However, to this day, I remain unclear regarding the exact cause of his affliction or the circumstances of his death. Nor was my own fragile condition as a boy ever mentioned. Apparently, my parents were just content that I had survived and, to outward appearance, was normal.

As a young child of seven, I remember believing that I had a line attached to the small of my back. This imaginary line with its endless capacity was anchored at the other end somewhere in my home. After I would venture out each day, I would try to take the exact path home. I was careful not to maneuver oddly and become wrapped around trees or buildings for fear of "getting my line tangled." I even created a rule to remedy the situation if it became too apparent that I could no longer control my path. According to my "line law," I could simply reach behind me, grab the line, lift it skyward, and flip it to untangle it. However, I was allowed to use this extreme maneuver only once each day. Most people, even Mom and Dad, thought my behavior was all too bizarre and inexplicable. Maybe this was a precursor to life itself. As much as we try to control our lives, the outside world does become more and more of a factor as we venture out and expand our boundaries.

When I was in second grade, a baby-sitter watched me after school each day until my parents came home from work. I loved to climb trees, and we had a beautiful oak tree in one corner of our front yard. One day I decided to play a trick on my baby-sitter by hiding. I climbed high up the big oak tree in my front yard, in order to enjoy what I considered to be the best view in town. I secured myself in my usual perch and, tired from a long school day and the arduous climb, promptly fell asleep. As one can imagine, my sitter grew frantic and called the police. I woke about an hour later to a vast commotion below. Carefully I descended. My days of climbing trees for the foreseeable future were put on hold.

Another vivid recollection was in third grade at my parochial school. One day my teacher grew very upset. He could not find his new pen. He asked our class if anyone had seen his pen or know its whereabouts. Timing is everything. Inadvertently I giggled at the wrong moment. He made me stand in front of the class and accused me of stealing. He was convinced I had taken the pen. As punishment, I was required to stay after school each day for a week. When his wife found the pen at home some days later, he simply announced to the class that it had been recovered, never apologizing. I was too embarrassed to tell my parents of the incident.

My parents, both highly educated, worked in managerial positions. Dad headed an insurance firm and Mom was a professor and chair of the history department at nearby Portland State University. I remember accompanying my mother along the Park blocks many times to her office at the upper end of campus. She was a firm believer that the student of history is the one best equipped to comprehend the future.

After grade school, I went on to Tualatin High. Throughout grade school and high school my behavior was consistent. I remained very shy, hardly noticed. A list of my achievements could easily have fit on a post-it note. I never liked being spotted out for any reason. Being singled out brought extreme emotional discomfort. Oddly enough, wearing anything around my neck caused great physical discomfort. Necklaces, turtle necks or even scarves were off limits as they seemed to give me that "closed-in feeling."

Regardless of my shy personality and demeanor, I was able to excel academically and earned an academic scholarship to Linfield College in McMinnville, Oregon. I decided to major in chemistry at the small, private school. My chances for success would vastly increase in a small-school environment with caring professors who could personally get to know me. My minor was psychology. My primary motivation for this coursework was a quest to find answers to my own questions, to better understand my own personality and the reason for my odd characteristics and traits, or in my case, a lack of desire to stand out.

My aspiration was to work in a small lab, where I would be able to see the results of my work at once and in black and white. I knew that I could succeed in this environment. In this atmosphere I could easily achieve while remaining under the radar, drawing no attention to myself. I feared attracting anyone's interest in advancing my career. I did not wish to be forced out of my protective shell, even to collaborate through a team approach. I especially feared being asked to contribute in any way as a spokesperson.

Shortly after I turned twenty-one, I received my first

jury-duty summons. The legal process had always intrigued me. While in the courtroom, I was overcome by a very strange sensation, which I chalked up to social jitters. My heart started racing. I was gripped and then paralyzed by fear. The strong sensation I felt at the court hearing left me reeling. Luckily, I was eliminated quite early as a juror from the proceedings, a murder trial, and kept from any further embarrassment. I was immensely relieved. I would not have the awesome responsibility to decide the life-or-death fate of another human being.

After graduation, my goal and desire to work in a research lab became a reality. I was hired to work in the lab for Cures Corporation in Beaverton, Oregon. I felt privileged to work under the direction of the highly renowned Dr. Lee Gibbons. A brilliant man, he was well respected by his peers. Dr. Gibbons had previously been affiliated with Portland State University and knew my mother quite well. He had written several books and had published in many scholarly journals. He encouraged me to pursue a master's degree. I knew I had a lot to learn, but I also felt that, under the right tutelage, I could make a notable contribution to science.

Using innovative research studies and creative ideas, we worked hard each day in an effort to identify and isolate genes in the hope of finding answers and all-important cures. We worked in tandem with the NIH, the National Institutes of Health, in Bethesda, Maryland. Our corporation was extremely honored to assist the NIH, whose mission was to prevent disease and improve health through scientific integrity. This powerful and notable organization was very much our big brother and gave voice to our work. Our constant "background" or supportive position on projects took the pressure off me and lessened any potential chance for the spotlight. Simply put, I was free to experiment and contribute and would never be asked to present any results. Dr. Gibbons would take care of the rest. I could work hard in the name of science and never be required to articulate my observed findings. I had the best of both worlds.

My reality and sense of stability all changed on March 23, 2011. What began as a-play-by-the-book effort to study and identify the components of a certain group of human genes turned into a whirlwind ride towards self-realization proceeding far beyond my wildest dreams. It was a pivotal point that challenged me to look at life in an entirely different way, quite different from my regimented, scientific approach. I was requested to study a specific group of cells that determine DNA and to try to determine a biological relationship to *agoraphobia*, a social-panic disorder driven by the fear of losing control in public situations. In short, I unlocked the door to a new world—my world—and a world I had no idea even existed.

One Monday morning, at our regularly scheduled staff meeting, the normally calm, reserved Dr. Lee grew animated. He turned to me and smiled. "We've been handed a clinical trial that will require our undivided attention for the next few months. I am putting you in charge," he said. "There are some set methodologies which we must adhere to. However, as always, you are free to come up with your own systems and procedures."

With this vote of confidence, I earnestly began to study the dreaded disease and its effect on families and society. Agoraphobia, related to fear, is estimated to occur in 3.2 million adults in America. It affects more than 2% of adults from ages eighteen to fifty-four years of age. Agoraphobia isn't specific to any racial, ethnic or socioeconomic group, but, oddly, it is more than twice as likely to occur in women as in men. It seems to develop more often in late adolescence to early adulthood. As I researched more, I learned that this ailment can cause individuals to become extremely anxious when faced with certain public situations, especially if they have no avenue of escape. Repeated avoidance of such situations only reinforces the disease. Victims with panic attacks experience symptoms that can include shortness of breath, inability to swallow, sweating, heart palpitations, chest pain, possible dizziness, and an overall negative mood. The degree can vary from slight nervousness to a losing of control and can even feel as severe as a heart attack.

Many researchers believe that agoraphobia can be traced to a specific earlier life event. As a result, agoraphobia can limit future lifetime achievements and can lead to a depressed state of mind. Left untreated, it most likely will not go away.

The more I studied this disease, the more I could relate to and identify with its symptoms. I, too, was most likely a sufferer of agoraphobia. As each day went by, I became more and more convinced that the symptoms I was studying were consistent with my personal experience. Already I had begun a process of self-reflection which had unlocked a door to my own personality. This bizarre irony motivated me to assert myself even more.

After sifting through reams of paperwork and spending long hours researching the subject, I felt confident to start working with the physical evidence that the NIH had asked us to examine. As some believed that agoraphobia was tied to a genetic component, for the next several months I engaged in the laborious process of investigating hair follicles. I painstakingly analyzed the hair follicles of 100 non-agoraphobic donors versus 100 agoraphobic participants. Half of the agoraphobic donors would be taking a new drug called Mahlahment, discovered in Hawaii about eight months earlier. The name of the drug was derived from the Hawaiian word for "calm" and the Latin suffix "ment", meaning "act or condition of." So the meaning of the drug name, Mahlahment, seemed quite fitting, the act or condition of being calm. The purpose of the drug was to reduce agoraphobic symptoms by creating a sense of calmness.

On day thirty-four, after spending hours in the lab checking and rechecking my calculations, I made an appointment with Dr. Lee to discuss my findings.

"Dr. Lee, I seem to be coming up with an interesting pattern with the agoraphobic patients' samples," I offered.

"Adam, tell me. Don't be shy. There is no right or wrong answer," he asserted.

I nodded. "Yes, sir. Dr. Lee, as you are well aware, it has

been hypothesized that humans have a genetic location on Chromosome 3 that manages a person's risk for developing agoraphobia. After taking Mahlahment for 3 months, the site on Chromosome 3 of the agoraphobic donors is now virtually identical to that of the non-agoraphobics. Additionally, the results for the agoraphobic patients who did not take Mahlahment remain precisely the same. I think this is a significant preliminary breakthrough not only for Mahlahment but, more importantly, for agoraphobia."

Dr. Lee smiled. "Adam, if what you say is true, this could indeed point to a useful scientific break-through. But we need to be absolutely sure before we can release these findings. I will need some time to thoroughly review your findings."

"Yes sir. I completely understand."

With my work temporarily on hold with the agoraphobia project, I turned my time and attention to my previous project I had put on the back burner. Once again I became consumed in my work. Time passed quickly. It was more than three weeks before Dr. Lee called me into his office to provide me with an update on his review of my work on the agoraphobia project.

"Adam," he started, "I checked and re-checked your work and can confirm that your methodology and findings appear to be legitimate. I've asked another of my colleagues, Dr. Nancy Peterson, to check the data as well. Dr. Peterson has reached the same conclusions as you, and believes that this may be a significant breakthrough. I've already been in contact with the NIH and have sent them the data. Mahlahment may now be a candidate for the fast track. They want us to come to Bethesda, to meet with them and discuss our findings in person."

He looked me directly in the eye.

"This could be big Adam, very big. You have made an important contribution. Your findings may change the course of future treatment for agoraphobics. I insist that you take the credit for this scientific discovery and assume the role of lead investigator on the project. As such, you will be required to present these findings at the quarterly meeting in Bethesda. You will be paired with Cindy Parsons. Ms. Parsons is renowned for her work with phobias. She has a master's degree in psychology with an emphasis on phobias. I understand she is a very bright and pleasant woman. I took the liberty of inviting her to lunch today."

He continued. "However, after she accepted, a meeting was added to my schedule. Unfortunately, I will not be able to join you. Please offer my apology to Ms. Parsons. Take her out for a nice, leisurely lunch. Take some time. Get to know her. Bond with her. You both must become a strong, cohesive team. Since you will be working together on this project, it will be in your best interest. Oh, and before I forget to tell you, don't forget to keep your lunch receipt. You will need it for your expense report. I will make sure you are reimbursed."

With that said, he extended a hand. "Great work Adam," he said. "I am very proud of you."

I felt like the wind had been knocked out of me. I gasped. Presentation? I can't do a presentation! The thought resonated over and over in my mind. Yes, I should have been ecstatic about the vote of confidence and promotion to lead investigator, but my fears overshadowed any hope of enjoying my success. I couldn't foresee ever delivering a speech to the NIH, a group of such reputation and notoriety. There was no way I could accept this proposal. The few times in the past I had attempted public speaking, I had been terrible. The audience had been only my teachers and fellow students in my small classes at Linfield. I vividly recalled the light-headedness, the intense sweats, and feeling as if someone were choking the air out of me. I was afraid of screwing up at the expense of being viewed negatively and perceiving the public humiliation to follow. I remembered how embarrassed I was. I never wanted to be in that position again.

Fast forward: Here I was, poised to receive potential acclaim for a discovery along with career advancement. Instead of rejoicing, I found myself plotting an escape, contriving a plausible sickness or injury. My thoughts raced to extremes. Maybe I could find another job in the next two weeks? Furthermore, the thought of being alone with an unknown "Ms. Parsons" for lunch was downright scary. I lacked social skills. I didn't date. I was the guy who went to only one prom in four years of high school, an awkward date fashioned by my mother with the help of an associate's daughter who felt sorry for me. Yes, Amanda had made it crystal clear that we would be going only as friends!

The receptionist called me promptly at 11:45 a.m. to announce the arrival of Ms. Parsons. I took a deep breath, gathered myself, and headed for the lobby. There I spied an attractive, blonde haired woman. She appeared to be about 5'8" tall and clad in a beautifully tailored suit. As I approached, she stood. "You must be Adam," she said. She stuck out a hand and shook mine firmly. "I am so pleased to meet you. There's been a lot of buzz at the NIH regarding your work. Congratulations! I can't wait to hear more about it!"

"Thanks Ms. Parsons, I just got lucky. The specimens that I was given to analyze told a compelling story. The results jumped out, they would have been hard to miss."

"Please call me Cindy."

"Okay, Cindy. Dr. Lee was called into a meeting and will be unable to join us today. He asked me to extend his apology. Are you hungry? I'll drive since I know the area. Hopefully, we can still beat the lunch crowd."

We drove to a local restaurant. Along the way she touched on her deep familiarity with agoraphobia and social phobias. I couldn't help but notice how pretty and outgoing she was. Glumly it came to me: We would sure be the 'odd couple' on that stage.

The lunch was pleasant. Cindy did most of the talking. She was brilliant. Because of her extensive background and work in the area of phobias and psychology, the NIH had chosen her to co-present along with me. She would provide an overview of the work in this area and focus on the mental aspects. Our presentation was to be a combination of science and psychology. I would discuss my scientific findings and their potential impact. Cindy would discuss heredity, culture, the environment, and current advances in helping people overcome agoraphobia. I would furnish more pure data. We would present two differing views, from two disciplines poles apart.

We decided to meet once more to coordinate our roles and the information for our presentation before heading to Maryland. Since she lived in Corvallis and worked in the psychology department at Oregon State University, she was easily within driving distance. I would drive down since she had generously driven up the first time. I didn't mention that I still lived with my parents and that my polished Taurus actually belonged to my dad!

On Saturday, I met Cindy at the site of her choice, a sports bar and grill on the OSU campus. Although it was a Saturday, she was dressed neatly, in business casual attire. I was glad I had decided at the last minute to wear my khaki slacks and a dress shirt instead of my usual Saturday attire, jeans and t-shirt.

We had a wonderful dinner. She told me about her family. She had been born in the state of Washington, but had moved to Corvallis when she was ten. Her parents were retired. Her brother was an airline pilot. She had attended Lewis and Clark, another small college in Portland, as an undergraduate. She received a master's in psychology from

OSU with special emphasis in phobic disorders. There she decided to stay and work. She was an ardent Beaver football fan.

"I am just hopelessly single and married to my work," she summed. "What about you?"

Her words surprised me. "You could probably say the same thing about me, I haven't dated since college," I offered, stretching the truth. Actually, the college date had been a study session. A professor had assigned study partners and a co-ed and I had gone to the library to do research!

As the evening wore on, boisterous laughter from fellow patrons and the glare and blare of the televisions all around us made it very difficult for us to communicate. At once Cindy smiled, and suggested we depart for her condo, where it would be quieter. "I have a huge dining room table where we can spread out all of our materials," she offered.

I nodded. Yes, I would love to get out of this loud, raucous bar. I wondered if this would constitute a date, but certainly kept that thought to myself.

Her home, in an attractive part of Corvallis, was neat and orderly. Beautiful, large trees lined the street and the entrance to the condominium complex. We worked in her living room. She seemed much more organized and better prepared than I was, and would be much easier on the eyes. When my turn to speak came, I was a little nervous even in this rehearsal, but her positive reinforcement with comments such as "Excellent job!" and "Love it!" propelled me and provided boosts of courage. She made me believe that *I could* actually do this.

When we finished, Cindy turned to me and asked, "Adam, do you like chocolate chip cookies?"

My eyes widened. "Absolutely," I replied.

"I made a batch first thing this morning. I'll be right back."

She eased up, and within a few minutes returned with the cookies and some piping hot chocolate to wash them down. We munched, talked, and laughed. After about an hour, I stood up, shrugged that it was time for me to leave. Cindy furnished me more than enough cookies for the ride back. We would meet at the airport early on Saturday and fly together. As I drove home, my worry about the speech was being eroded by a desire to see Cindy again. It seemed crazy! I approached everything from a concrete, black and white, scientific perspective, while Cindy viewed the world from the very opposite end of the spectrum. Her softer psychological perspective helped her view issues from a variety of viewpoints. Differences aside, for the first time in my life I felt like I could finally relate to someone. I found it so ironic that Cindy wasn't someone from an "exact science" discipline. For a fleeting moment came a flicker of hope.

Dr. Lee was pleased by my enthusiasm with the project. Apparently, he had never met Cindy! He told me that he would be leaving for Maryland on Friday, a day before us. We would meet at the conference before our presentation.

On Saturday, we met as planned. She looked as pretty as ever. We chatted comfortably together on the flight and upon arriving grabbed a shuttle to the luxurious Hyatt Regency Hotel in downtown Bethesda. Our rooms were extravagant. Cindy and I agreed to meet in the lobby an hour before our presentation.

In the foyer of the conference area stood Dr. Lee. He wished us good luck. I took a moment and introduced him to Cindy. She was sporting a very striking red dress with coordinating red shoes. I was in a navy-blue suit with a red striped tie. Although we had not previously discussed our attire, we actually coordinated.

After two speakers, it was our turn to take the stage. I remember my name was called and dazedly I rose and mechanically moved toward the podium. I looked down from the stage and out toward the large audience, then peeked back to Cindy who gave me a smile. I cleared my throat and attempted to speak from my notes. However, my voice was not audible. I quickly panicked. Suddenly I was gasping for air and I felt a great pressure around my neck. My heart began to pound overwhelmingly. I grew dizzy. I felt like I was having a heart attack. I could see the crowd fidgeting and hear them mumbling before me. I wiped my forehead, by now soaked with perspiration. I wanted to run off the stage as fast as I could. I just wanted to be left alone. I thought I had adequately prepared myself again and again for this moment. I guess I was foolish to believe that I could really get up on stage and deliver a speech. But hadn't we rehearsed, carefully, at least a dozen times? I was devastated and felt publicly humiliated. How ironic, I thought. I had worked so diligently to uncover the cause of agoraphobia, and now had found myself frozen on stage, a victim of the same dreaded disease.

I stood, in a daze, with nowhere to hide. At once I felt a tug on my arm and a hand on my back and being escorted off the stage. After a brief moment, I could hear Cindy speaking as I sat in the wings, just behind the curtain. Her voice fell, then sounded again distantly, apologizing for us both. She told the audience that I had fallen extremely ill on the flight and convincingly told the crowd how much she admired me for attempting to deliver the speech under these conditions. There came a prolonged burst of applause for Cindy. Not only had she presented her part magnificently, but from memory she skillfully articulated the highlights of my work. As if this weren't enough, she assured the audience how fortunate agoraphobia was to have me as a dedicated scientist and researcher. More applause erupted.

After, Dr. Lee didn't speak to me or even look my way. I could tell he was angry, and it was probably justified. I knew that I let him down. Cindy pulled him aside and talked to him for a few minutes. Whatever she said seemed to calm him down considerably. He nodded and then left without a word. Cindy quickly approached with a smile.

"Hey, I don't know about you, but I'm starving! Let's get out of here and get a nice dinner. I won't take no for an answer. Besides, I need a date and I don't know anyone from Maryland."

Her words were assuring and made me smile. I rose to

my feet. During dinner Cindy never mentioned the speech. Instead, she seemed very upbeat. She spoke to me like an old, close friend. I felt undeserving of the attention and a little embarrassed. We enjoyed a leisurely dinner and talked for at least an hour afterwards, over dessert and a cup of coffee. After, I walked Cindy to her room. "Cindy, I want to thank you for a wonderful night," I said. "I'm sorry I let you down and left you out on a limb. Very sorry."

Cindy smiled. "Adam, please don't mention it. You are my colleague, my friend. I had to help. That's what friends do. They take care of each other. Besides, you have so much going for you. You just need to believe in your abilities. I believe in you, and I know you much better than anyone in that audience. Thanks for a lovely dinner. It was fun." With that, she gave me a little wink and a pat on the arm.

We said good night. As I lay in bed staring up, I kept thinking how lucky I had been to run into Cindy! Somehow with incredible timing, an angel had appeared in my life. Yes, she had come at exactly the right time.

Chapter Two

The next morning Cindy and I flew out together. She seemed quiet on the plane and actually slept a good part of the flight. We hugged goodbye at the Portland airport and went our separate ways. I didn't know if I would ever see her again, but I hoped I would.

The rest of the weekend flew by quickly. On Monday morning Dr. Lee seemed his usual self at first, but later he asked me to meet him in his office for a brief meeting at 10:00 a.m. I caught up on my email and was pleasantly surprised to receive a message from Cindy. She told me she had enjoyed the trip to Maryland and thanked me for joining her for dinner. I quickly replied and thanked her again, for all she had done for me.

At ten I met Dr. Lee in his office. After I had sat down, he closed the door. For a moment he sat by, quiet, downright pensive. Then he spoke. "Adam, I have a very high opinion of you. I have known your mother for years; you come from a wonderful family. You are very talented, but I am concerned about the anxiety that you demonstrated. It affected your ability to deliver your presentation. I want to help you." With that, he rose from his chair and walked around his desk. Leaning against its edge, he proposed, "Adam, I want you to see Mrs. Nelson, the Human Resources Manager. She is aware of what happened in Maryland. We have discussed the incident and are eager to find resources for you to become a more confident and productive employee. Adam, if you can jump this hurdle, your potential will be limitless. You have nothing to lose, everything to gain. What do you think?"

"Dr. Lee, I want to apologize for what happened in Maryland. I didn't mean to embarrass you or the company. I wish I could wave a wand and change who I am or overcome whatever is stopping me in my tracks. I'll gladly meet with Mrs. Nelson."

Dr. Lee stood and shook my hand, and patted me on the back. "Adam, I really do enjoy working with you. Mrs. Nelson will be in touch later today. In the meantime, I know that I can count on you to continue the outstanding work that you have consistently demonstrated in the lab. Thanks for your cooperation."

It was shortly after lunch that Mrs. Nelson contacted me and suggested we meet. I walked the short distance to her office. She was an attractive woman in her late fifties. In a very business-like manner she provided a synopsis of what had occurred at the conference. I nodded, verifying her version.

"Adam, we are here to help you. This anxiety you feel needs attention. I want you to consider seeing a psychologist named Dr. Morris. He has done a great deal of work in this area. I took the liberty to check his availability. Fortunately, he had a cancellation today and if you are in agreement, he will see you at four this afternoon. What do you think?"

"Thank you for setting up the appointment. That will work out fine," I said quietly.

The rest of the day was a blur. At 3:55 I found myself in Dr. Morris' waiting room. Plaques adorned the walls. Dr. Morris had a Ph.D. in psychology and appeared to be very successful. Precisely at four, Dr. Morris appeared in the waiting room to greet me. A very cordial man, he walked me into his office.

Once I was settled, he began to question me at great length about my medical history, family, and experiences. He asked me if I could identify the source of my discomfort. I shared that being singled out in any way led to extreme emotional discomfort. I discussed the uneasy feelings I had experienced at jury duty. As for physical discomforts, I told him that I couldn't tolerate wearing anything around my neck. Jewelry, turtlenecks and even scarves were off limits as they gave me that "closed-in feeling" and the sensation of being choked.

He asked me to tell him more about the incident in Maryland and what might have led up to it. I told him again that I had always been extremely reserved and shy and always tried to stay under the radar, in essence, to remain invisible. Any attention in my direction had always bothered me, most of my life. Then he asked me to describe the precise sequence of events on that particular day. I narrated the specifics as best I could, culminating with Cindy gently ushering me off the stage. "I don't know what I would have done without her help," I concluded.

"You are a very lucky person to have a companion like Cindy watching over you," he declared. Then he continued. "If it is in fact agoraphobia, it is not easily treated. Medications can help. Some psychotherapy can be effective. Many times an earlier life event can trigger an episode, and finding that particular event is the key. If you do have a special friend like Cindy or someone you really trust, you need to enlist them. I have been down this road many times. You need to have someone you can lean on, who can provide you safety, and most of all, trust. Adam, this is critical. Take some time and think about this. It's pivotal to successful treatment."

During the last part of our session, Dr. Morris administered a test to determine my possible phobias. The results were readily available for his analysis. With the procedure complete and my results in hand, he sat back, took a deep breath, and then concluded.

"Adam, based on the results of your test and the information you've provided me, I think that you need to see a specialist. Factoring these, along with the length of time you have had this condition leads me to believe that there may be a deep-seated reason why you have not outgrown it. It's also remotely possible that you may have an underlying medical condition exacerbating the situation."

Dr. Morris scribbled down some information, then handed me a card.

"Adam, I want you to see a friend of mine, Dr. Billings. He is a psychiatrist and a fellow Yale grad. He's very well known and will be able to get to the bottom of this much faster than anyone."

Together we stood. Again Dr. Morris shook my hand, then looked me straight in the eye, "Good luck Adam," he said. "Don't worry. Dr. Billings will get to the bottom of this."

Anxious to get moving, I pulled out Dr. Billings' business card the moment I got home. Noting that he had office hours late on Tuesdays, I called to make an appointment. I was greeted by a pleasant receptionist, who scheduled me for the following Tuesday. The next day I received another email from Cindy. She had a meeting in Portland on Tuesday and wondered if I would be available for dinner afterward. My appointment with Dr. Billings was at four, but we would have plenty of time. Without hesitation, I agreed and said that it would be wonderful to see her again. She emailed a suggestion that we meet at an Italian restaurant in Washington Square at 5:30. I agreed. I respected her and enjoyed her company, but almost at once I felt some goosebumps.

The week flew by. For the greater part of the week, I had a lingering nervous flutter in my stomach. I wasn't quite sure if it was because of the upcoming session with Dr. Billings or the dinner date with Cindy. Either way, I felt pressure, enormous and building.

Tuesday I left work a few minutes early to insure that I would be on time for my appointment. Dr. Billings was very cordial. He started with a thorough medical exam, then drew a blood panel to send to the lab. The results would be available in two days. Already Dr. Billings had reviewed the clinical notes from his colleague, Dr. Morris. Once again, he pointed out the importance of having a very close friend or confidant as I journeyed down the treatment path.

"If in fact you are affected by agoraphobia, it has to do

with fear and panic," he said. "And it is best to have someone who can assist you in your progress. However, I am not yet prepared to make a diagnosis of agoraphobia. Social phobia, something that I can't rule out for now, has very similar symptoms. Agoraphobia is a fear of public or extremely open areas, whether they include people or not. Social phobia is the fear of actual interaction with other people."

I was asked to recount, yet once more, the entire sequence of events, on that dreadful day in Maryland, followed by some intense questioning about my childhood and past. The doctor seemed to be looking for a significant past experience that might be the root cause of my condition. I told him about the pen in third grade, my issues in college, my jury duty, and other such memories through the years.

At once he leaned back and nodded. "Adam, from my experience I don't think it is one of these occurrences that is causing your problem. This is much more than the need to join a Toastmasters group. There is something here that you and I can't put our fingers on. Let's wait for the results of your lab tests, before we jump to conclusions and formulate a treatment plan. But I must tell you this. I am leaning toward regression analysis as the next logical step."

I looked at him, "Regression analysis?" I asked.

"Yes, Adam, regression analysis. Let me tell you about it. It begins by putting you in a hypnotic state. Hypnosis is used for many problems such as alcoholism, excess weight, smoking, depression, insomnia, pain, and numerous phobias. When a person has a deep-seated problem, regression analysis is often times used as a technique that uncovers the explanation and root cause. Most of us have experienced meeting a stranger whom we seem to already know or being in a location 'all too familiar.' Many refer to these as déjà vu experiences. Unconsciously, people carry information from prior lives and bring it with them into current lives. This information can include people we have formerly known, experiences we have had, and perhaps places we have been. Many of us carry deep emotional baggage. Memories of our past are stored in incredible detail in our subconscious. Because they are stored there, our fears include a lack of understanding. If a person has a traumatic experience or something left unresolved in an earlier lifetime, this can remain in his memory and be carried forward to affect the present lifetime. Records from our past are stored in our unconscious and sometimes start to resound negatively, to breed phobias and relationship issues in our new lives. These memories are why and how we fashion our current existences, as we do and are the root of our belief system."

He continued. "Past life therapy is the process of going back to the original place where we experienced a significant particular event. I will attempt to do this with hypnosis and guided imagery. As we go back in time, I will try to help you re-experience a certain event in your prior life. By understanding the significance and the impact of this experience, we can go forward with open minds to deal with the issue at hand. If we find great fear in an earlier life, we *must* distinguish this fear as related and *release* it. However, it must be the same *exact* fear. You see Adam, all of the answers we are looking for are within you."

"If they're within me, how will you find them?" I asked.

"Great question, Adam. During the process you will be in a relaxed state, similar to dreaming. This will allow you to easily recognize images, symbols, and signs as we attempt to uncover the secrets from your past. You will be aware of sounds and sensations and will be open to growth and change. Many times people don't feel any different during hypnosis and, as a result, are unsure about the information they elicit. The first emotion that surfaces during the journey of your mind is usually the most significant and should be the one to consider. I don't know if you have ever meditated, Adam, but between now and our session try to spend at least one-half hour each day doing so. You will benefit greatly, because people in a relaxed state tend to be more successful with regression. Ultimately, your self-esteem will improve and you will be personally empowered. Having done this, I believe you will be successful."

I was now starting to wrestle with the notion that past life regression meant multiple lives. Apparently this was a process predicated on a belief in reincarnation. I had never even considered such a phenomenon. For now, I felt it would be best not to rock the boat and keep my skepticism to myself.

With that, we concluded our session. Assuming the results of my lab tests would lie within normal limits, I scheduled a 90-minute regression analysis for the following

Tuesday.

It didn't take me long to drive to Washington Square. Actually I was a few minutes early. Within ten minutes Cindy entered the lobby, clad in an overcoat accented by a bright red scarf around her neck.

"Hi Adam, how have you been?" she inquired.

"Pretty good," I answered. "Pretty good."

"I hope you are hungry. I have some good news I want to share it with you," she said as she smiled magnificently at me.

We were led to a corner booth not far from a cheerily lit fireplace. "This will be great, thank you," she said to the hostess as we took our seats. She laid her purse and coat on one of the vacant chairs. She was wearing a long-sleeved emerald green dress.

"Do you like my new dress?" she asked with a grin.

"Very pretty, Cindy. Very." It was all I could muster.

The waiter approached to take our drink order. Cindy asked if I would like to split a bottle of wine. I agreed.

With that she sat back, smiled and said, "Guess what Adam?"

I smiled back, "What?"

"Two months ago I submitted an article to an A-list magazine on phobias. I just came from my meeting in Portland. The editor advised me that they are going to publish it. Best of all, I am going to be paid very well for the article. So in about a month I will officially 'be published.' Want to know the best part? They want me to continue doing monthly feature articles. Isn't that great?"

"That's wonderful news. Wonderful. I am really happy for you, you deserve it."

"Thanks Adam. I just wanted to celebrate and share the good news with someone. My parents are out of state. My brother is in Baltimore. Honestly, I was hoping you might be able to assist me down the road when I get stuck on some of the more technical science issues. Which I will."

"Thanks for asking, I'll be willing to help in any way I can."

I raised my glass, "To Cindy, the new up-and-coming feature writer and to her amazing flare with the pen!"

Cindy lifted her glass and smiled in return.

We ordered our dinners. I don't know if it was the wine or the fire or Cindy's energetic company that encouraged me to start conversing more than usual. I began to open up and found myself talking much, much more than usual. I even divulged my work issue. Cindy promised to keep it confidential and encouraged me to go.

"Adam," she started. "I'm proud that you are following through. This is an important step. I know a great deal about phobias and I think I can help you. Right now, more than anything you need a person willing to listen to you and walk with you on this path. If you can find someone to trust, the odds are far better. I'll be willing to be that person for you, Adam. I really want to see you beat this thing."

I was stunned. I had known her for less than a month, yet I really trusted her. For the first time in my life I felt I had found a true friend.

"I really appreciate the offer, Cindy. I value you as a true friend, and I'd love to take you up on it. Thank you very much."

Cindy suggested that we either chat or meet at least once a week. She also recommended that I keep a notebook to record my thoughts and chart my progress. I thought the idea was a very helpful suggestion. I could really see the value in keeping a notebook journal. The results would be documented in black and white!

"See, Adam? There can be a happy medium between science and psychology," she played.

We laughed heartily.

After dinner, we shared a tasty tiramisu for dessert. We must have talked for over an hour before I delicately reminded her that she had an hour drive ahead of her. Soon I was walking her to her car and thanking her for a most wonderful evening. This time I was the one who gave a little pat on the shoulder.

"Congratulations again on the article, Cindy, I am proud of you. Very proud. And thanks again for being my friend and for letting me confide in you."

"I am proud to be your friend, Adam. I expect an update next week," she said, flashing her signature smile. With that, she rolled up the window and drove off into a light mist.

It had been a wonderful evening, the best of my life. Maybe I could lick this thing, especially with a friend like Cindy alongside me? Next Tuesday would be my second step, a step back in time with the hope for a better future.

Chapter Three

By Tuesday I was warming to the idea of my next session with Dr. Billings and undergoing regression analysis. After all, maybe the procedure would yield some deep-seated secret I needed to come to grips with and rid me of these panic attacks. While the whole idea of regression seemed too New Age for me with my anal, scientific background, Cindy had said it well: "We must always remain open-minded to truly understand our existence."

I arrived a few minutes early for my session. I had changed into clothes a little more comfortable on the advice of Dr. Billings. Cindy had suggested and I had confirmed with the office that my session would be taped.

Dr. Billings came out to greet me at preciously five. We walked back to his office where he gestured for me to sit in a recliner chair. He then began to explain.

"Adam, I want to put you in a state of mind where you will be more likely to accept my suggestions. In this state, your subconscious will be more readily accessible. You will not be asleep. Rather, you will have a keen sense of awareness. You will be very cognizant of your surroundings. Above all, I want you to relax. A relaxed state is the essence of hypnosis. Don't worry, a therapist cannot make you do anything against your will. I can only suggest thoughts. However, if a suggestion is unacceptable, your ego or sense of self will protect you and reject the suggestion. A good way to envision this state of mind, Adam, is to think of it as a daydream. Here you will be in an altered state but will be able to react and respond as necessary."

He cleared his throat, took pause, and resumed, "Adam, I need a basis on which to start. It might be best for me to analyze and enter your subconscious possibly from authority figures, humiliations, or even family relationships. Based on what you have told me so far and my gut feeling, I am going to approach the situation from the aspect of shyness. When did Adam first become a shy individual?"

I said nothing.

"Since you already look comfortable, I am going to induce a deeper relaxation. We want to activate those memories unknown under normal circumstances. Close your eyes. Begin by taking several very slow, deep breaths. Breathe each in, then slowly breathe it out. As you do so, Adam, imagine yourself becoming very calm and serene. As you continue to breathe in and out, think of the word RELAX again and again. Make sure that you are comfortable. Pick a spot on the ceiling, one of the plaster swirls or the light fixture, whichever is comfortable. I'm going to count down from five to one. When I say ONE you'll be in a deep level of relaxation. Just allow the process to take place effortlessly, easily. You're in your mind now, your unconscious mind. Focus on the spot and focus on your breathing, your breath is going in and out. Again, focus on your breathing. And FIVE ... allow yourself to relax, effortlessly and easily. Each breath in, each breath out ... and each number down. And FOUR. Notice how your eyelids are blinking more and more and growing heavier and heavier. Whenever you're ready, and because you can, go ahead and close your eyes. Allow the process to take place effortlessly, easily. Your eyes are closing and becoming heavier and heavier. Continue to relax. You'll notice that the calm feeling continues to grow as you continue to relax, deeper and deeper, more and more with each breath in, each breath out. Each number down and THREE ... Just taking your inner eye now, your unconscious eye, and focus on your body, on the inside, and search for any tension in your body. If there is any, just take a deep breath and blow it out. Notice your face and your neck and your shoulders. Notice your upper back, your upper chest, your upper arms releasing tension. If there is tension, just blow it out. That's right, noticing how comfortable that is. Noticing your mid-back, your mid-chest, lower back and lower abdomen, lower arms and wrists and fingers. If there is any tension at all, just take a deep breath and blow it out. As you relax, your breathing becomes nice and smooth and helps you relax. Noticing your waist, your hips, your buttocks and your pelvic area in the front and the back ... and if there is any tension, continue to take deep breaths and blow it out. Noticing your knees, your shins, the calves of your legs and ankles. If there is any tension, take a deep breath and blow it out. Noticing your feet now, your toes, the balls of your feet. If there is any tension, just blow it out. That's right, just notice how comfortable you are as you continue to relax. More and more you notice the heaviness on your eyelids continue to grow. Your eyelids are so very, very heavy as you continue to relax, deeper and deeper. More and more and

TWO, taking your inner eye and unconscious eye ... noticing your body from the top of your head to the bottom of your feet, noticing your body becoming heavier and heavier or lighter and lighter and whichever that is ... heaviness or lightness, noticing it as you continue. When I say ONE you will be all the way down to a deep level of relaxation. And ONE ... Be there NOW in mind, body, and spirit.

Now using your inner eyes, your unconscious eyes, you notice yourself standing there. When you notice yourself standing there, turn around in the opposite direction. When you turn around you will notice that you are standing across from a room and the door is open. Just go ahead and walk to the room and look in, noticing the light coming in through the window, noticing the furniture in the room. Go ahead and walk into the room. As you enter the room, look around. Notice everything. Noticing if the walls are wall papered or painted. Noticing the colors. Noticing if there is anything on the walls. Noticing the furniture. Then look around and find a comfortable place to sit. And go ahead and sit down. Noticing how peaceful and quiet this room is. I'm going to count from three to one. When I say ONE you will be back to the time and place when "SHYNESS" first entered the soul's energy. Just going back ... to that time and that place. And THREE ... just noticing a kaleidoscope of images and faces and going all the way back in time. That's right ... and TWO and noticing that the images, faces, and places are slowing down. Just noticing now how when I say ONE you will be able to notice exactly where you are and what's going on all the way back to that time and that place when SHYNESS entered the soul's energy. That's right. And ONE. Be there now in mind, body, and spirit. Now in a clear, audible voice just tell me what's going on? What's coming up?"

"I can see my surroundings. A woven chair. I'm in a small room. Very, very, simple. The walls are plain. Very plain."

"Besides the woven chair, what other furniture is there?"

"When I first opened the door, I thought I saw a couch and a woven chair. Now I don't see a couch. I see just a woven chair."

"So are you standing in the room?"

"No, I am seated in the chair."

"You are seated in the woven chair?"

"Yes."

"Notice your feet. What you are wearing on your feet?"

"I am wearing sandals."

"When you look at the sandals, how are they held on your feet?"

"There are straps that come across."

"What else are you wearing?"

"I have a dress on."

"If you have a dress on, are you a male or female? Take your physical arms and put them across your chest to see if you are male or female."

"I'm ... a female."

"What's going on in your life?"

"I'm lonely."

"You're lonely. Does anyone else live there with you?"

"No."

"You're alone?"

"Yes, but I don't think this is a house."

"And what is it?"

"It's a room. There are windows on two of the walls. Small windows. One on each wall. Each window has two bars so you can't get in or out. The bars are inside the window."

"So are the bars vertical or horizontal?"

"Vertical."

"What is the color and shape of the bars?"

"The bars are brown and the walls are tan. They are circular."

"So what is the occasion that you are in this room?"

"I'm not sure, but I feel lonely."

"How old are you?"

"I'm elderly."

"So when you say elderly, what age does that mean?"

"Seventyish."

"What is your hair like?"

"I have a bun on my head."

"On the top or on the back?"

"In the back of my head."

"Can you go back one week and tell me what's going on? One week before you were sitting in the woven chair? Three ... two ... one ... Be there now. What's going on?"

"I'm in a house with a group of people. There's a lot of commotion, a lot of noise. It's like a home with a long table and a lot of chairs."

"Would it be a boarding house?"

"No, it's ... more formal, for some reason."

"Is it a family home?"

"It almost seems like it."

"Is this like a family home with a lot of relatives around?"

"Yes, there are a lot of people."

"And so at this big table are you having a meal?"

"No."

"Go back to a time when there was a meal at that big table ... Three ... two ... one ... Be there now. Okay, what do you see?"

"There are many of the same people."

"How many are there?"

"Around twenty."

"When you are there, are you doing a lot of the talking?"

"No."

"Are you more of a spectator?"

"Yes."

"Are you sitting on the side or at the head of the table?"

"Right at the side. At the end. There's a man with a hat at the end of the table."

"What kind of a hat?"

"It's almost like a capotain."

"Look around the table. Is there anyone you recognize?"

"I have no feelings about who they are."

"Is there someone in the kitchen bringing food? Or was the food just brought out before everyone sat down?"

"There isn't any food anymore."

"The food is all eaten?"

"There wasn't any food. It wasn't there to begin with."

"Oh, there wasn't any food? Everyone sat down but there wasn't any food?"

"It's like I was supposed to be here for some reason. I was brought here."

"What's going on with the people sitting? Are they saying anything?"

"They seem very disgusted with me for some reason. There's a lot of talking going on."

"What are they talking about?"

"They're angry with me."

"Is everyone, across the board, negative toward you?"

"Yes. I don't fit in."

"What's the not-fitting-in part?"

"They are showing anger towards me."

"Across the board everyone is angry?"

"Yes. And I thought I was one of them."

"One of them ... What would that mean?"

"In their eyes, normal."

"Normal as in a member of the group?"

"Yes. I didn't realize I was different."

"How are you different?"

"I see things differently."

"Are there both men and women in the group?"

"Yes, and a few of the women are younger."

"Is the number of men to women fairly even?"

"There are many more men."

"What is this about?"

"A meeting."

"What's the meeting about?"

"Me. How to proceed with me and the others."

"How to proceed? What do you mean?"

"I'm not quite sure."

"Were you someone of authority once?"

"I'm not sure."

"Prior to coming to this meeting, what were you doing?"

"Just living my life."

"And where were you living your life?"

"At home. But I was tricked into coming to this meeting."

"Who tricked you?"

"A man I thought was a friend."

"He took you away?"

"Yes."

"And who are these people of such importance?"

"The heads of the town."

"And where's your husband? Is he in the meeting?"

"No. He's gone."

"So where would he be?"

"He's ... dead."

"So you are at this meeting and what is your understanding? Why are you at this meeting?"

"There's a lot of anger about me."

"What are they angry about?"

"I really can't tell you what they are saying. It's a feeling I am getting. It's as if one of the young girls is talking the other ones into it. Now I'm getting the feeling that four other women will be coming to this same kind of meeting."

"Mob mentality?"

"Yes."

"So there are about fifteen to twenty people? Why don't you just walk out?"

"They won't let me."

"They'll stop you?"

"Yes."

"And how are you aware that they will not let you leave?"

"There are men sitting next to me."

"What are they discussing and what are they angry about? Is it a tribunal?"

"It could be. I dress like them. I look like them. But my mind is different."

"They think your mind is different? They think you're crazy? What are they hinging that information on?"

"The words of the young girls. The way they see me carry myself. But I should be allowed to. I have the right. I'm not hurting anyone. I look at things differently, but that means nothing and hurts no one. I'm my own person. Because I'm honest in my beliefs, they don't appreciate me. If I was one of them, they would overlook this. But I'm not afraid to voice my opinion and it bothers them. They say it's evil. They don't know me."

"How do you feel right now?"

"I'm a good person. I don't perceive the situation the way they do. It's between God and me. I'm sad that my husband is not here to help me like he helped me before."

"What would you say is your personality?"

"Different. I do not give in to their lies. I pity them."

"When I say ONE, I'm going to move the story to a time when a conclusion takes place. We're moving ahead ... closer to modern times."

"Yes. From that room, I go back to the little room where I am sitting."

"Do you go there directly?"

"Yes. I'm waiting."

"What are you waiting for?"

"Them."

"Are you wearing the same clothes you wore at the big table?"

"Yes."

"So you didn't even get a change of clothes?"

"No."

"How do you feel?"

"It's ... over."

"What's over?"

"Living's not worth it any more. When people have such low opinions of you, you want to ... move on."

"You want to leave that room?"

"I want to move out of town quickly."

"Now move ahead to the next event. You are sitting in the room waiting and THREE, TWO, ONE. What's going on now?"

"They're escorting me out. Two men, one on each arm.

They're walking me down a path. I see horses."

"Horses? Are the horses walking around?"

"No, they're attached to a wagon."

"So are they taking you somewhere in the wagon?"

"Yes."

"And how are you sitting in the wagon?"

"I'm sitting down in the back."

"How are you seated?"

"Facing the back, away from the horses."

"Stay with the story."

"My hands are tied and there are two drivers, or one driver and one other. They are driving hastily. There are hills. People along the way are jeering at me and are scornful. They are going to hurt me now. I feel tears on my cheeks. We arrive on top of a hill. There are many, many people. Other carts arrive, with other women."

"There are a lot of people there?"

"Yes, many, many. They knew we were coming. Some are from the table. There are hundreds of others. They tie my hands behind me now. They are going to kill me."

"How are they going to kill you?"

"They are going to hang me."

"Where are they going to hang you?"

"From a tree. I pity them. I am the winner."

"How are you the winner?"

"Because God knows. God knows I am innocent. I will be in His house."

"Uh-huh. He sure does. Are you hanged? Are you dead?"

"I think I am!"

"Where is your soul?"

"Heaven."

"Your soul already went to heaven?"

"I believe it is in heaven."

"Let's go back to the hanging. THREE, TWO, ONE. Freeze-frame the picture. What's going on?"

"To where they are going to hang me?"

"Yes. Tell me the next thing that happens after they tie your hands behind your back."

"They take me from the wagon, lead me to the tree. They make me climb the ladder under a big limb."

"Do they put the rope around the limb?"

"No, it was already around the branch. The crowd is chanting and slandering me."

"Do they put a noose around your neck and kick the ladder out from under you?"

"Yes. I don't want to remember that, though. I just want to go from the wagon to the peaceful feeling."

"And that's what you do?"

"Yes. I don't want to think of that again."

"Now I'm going to freeze-frame the picture. What was your last thought? ONE ...The last thought you had ... Just close your eyes, take it easy. There you are ... take it easy. There was a last thought. What was that last thought? ONE."

"I am at peace."

"What was the thought right before the feeling of peace?"

"They have done it. They don't understand what they

have done. Someday they will."

"The soul has left the body? What goes on next?"

"Peace. Light. Calm."

"That's good."

"It's like it really doesn't matter what happened back there. It is just something I had to go through, live through."

"Okay, so go ahead. What is the next thing that your soul does? ONE ..."

"I'm a baby. I have my same two parents as I have right now. But it's not long after they were married. I feel I'm their first baby, Michael. My life is short. Very short. I will die in ... a dozen days."

"What is the cause of death?"

"There are issues. I know I have an additional toe on one foot."

"Crib death? SIDS?"

"No."

"Heart failure?"

"Yes, I think so."

"I'm not placed right with my parents or circumstances have changed. It isn't supposed to happen."

"What does your soul learn between its time as Michael and when you come back as Adam?"

"Timing is important."

"And several years later you reincarnate as Adam."

"Yes."

"What is foremost in your mind?"

"What people think of you is important. But what you

think of yourself is much more important. Be true to yourself. Have confidence. Don't worry. You have gone through more pain than anyone, and if you can live through that ... your present life is a piece of cake. You ... just need to take steps and believe in yourself."

"How is Adam doing now?"

"He's stuck in a rut. He needs to trust in God and things will work out. He can have all the reinforcement he wants all day long from others, but he has to believe in himself."

"So what is keeping him stuck? ONE ..."

"The past."

"Is it this lifetime or are other lives coming up that keep him stuck?"

"It might be just the one. Yes, just the one."

"Is there anything he needs to process."

"For some reason I feel like I am over that, but I'm too thin-skinned, I guess. Maybe I'm not. Maybe I'm just confused."

"No one is ever too thin-skinned Adam. That's a misnomer. We sometimes think that if we ignore our feelings we can navigate better. And in that lifetime of yours, she—I forgot to get her name—was disempowered to the nth degree Her power was taken from her for no good reason other than others were afraid of her. If nothing else, I'm going to ask the universe if it knows the name of that person."

"It almost feels like 'Susan,' but I'm not entirely sure," I offered.

"There may be some misplaced mockery. As we come

back to this part we can unravel all the pieces. I'd like to tell Susan how brave she is, the courage it took her to come back. Even though Michael stayed for such a short time, your soul returned as Adam to start over again. That is wonderful. And now Adam is going to get everything figured out so that everyone can feel empowered—all the way back to Susan. What's next for Susan?"

"I'm going to finally solve the problem."

"So is Susan feeling relieved that the problem will be solved?"

"Yes."

"Good. I want to thank those two entities, Susan and Michael, for appearing and acknowledging their roles in this story. Now we can sort out all the pieces and heal all the souls that need healing. When you hear this Adam, what comes up in your thoughts?"

"Love. Everyone sharing God's love."

"Yes, this will help everybody heal. All will be free to live in their eternities any way they please. No one will be stuck. No one will flounder. Everyone will be re-empowered to their God-given powers. Adam, bring your mind back to the time you first walked into the room and looked around."

"I'm there."

"How do you feel?"

"I feel relieved. This room isn't as dreadful as it seemed. It was such an important room then. Now it's ... rather meaningless."

"Notice how peaceful and quiet the room is now. Now

turn your head and walk out. When you're out let me know. Go ahead and turn around and bring your mind into this room, into this time and this space. When you notice yourself on the recliner, let me know."

"I'm there."

"I'm going to count from one to three. And when I say THREE you will be all the way back to the here and now, wide awake, refreshed, and relaxed. And ONE coming up, just allowing all the information to assemble in its own time, in its space. All the information will come to you for your well-being and your healing, and TWO, all the energy is coming up into your mind, your head, your hands, your feet. Bringing all the energy back up and THREE ... all the way back to the here and now. Wide awake, refreshed, and relaxed. Adam, you can open your eyes whenever you're ready."

I opened my eyes. My regression was over. Dr. Billings did not want to elaborate just yet. He wanted time to reflect and ponder on what he'd heard. He talked for another ten minutes about phobias and causes, about possible treatments, about next steps. "Adam," he said, "this session took a great deal out of you mentally and physically. Get some rest. Continue to meditate each day. Drink several glasses of water each day. I'll contact you by next week."

He was right, I was emotionally drained. It was a chore just to drive home. That night I discussed nothing with my parents and went to bed earlier than I had in years. I dozed off wondering if I had actually been hypnotized successfully.

Could it be possible that my responses were derived from another source other than my own subconscious? Or ... had I really lived before?

Chapter Four

Within a few days I called Cindy with an update. She seemed almost captivated as I related the details of my session with Dr. Billings. We scheduled our weekly meeting for Saturday in Corvallis. She asked me to bring along the recording from the session. She was eager, she said, to hear it firsthand.

That Saturday the skies opened up. I drove through a steady downpour the entire trip. With all this rain, I thought, no wonder Oregon is so lush and green. To me, it's well worth the inconvenience to enjoy nature's bounty the year around.

I arrived in the early afternoon. We would listen to and analyze the tape, then formulate an action plan. Cindy suggested that we work a few hours and then order a pizza. Afterwards, if needed, we could continue on. I was beginning to think she must be at least part Italian.

Before we listened to the tape, I decided to prep Cindy about Dr. Billings' beliefs about phobias, their causes, regression analysis, and possible remedies. The day after my session, with everything still fresh in my mind, I had written extensive notes about the process and what I had experienced. I had done some Net research so as not to overlook any vital information that could benefit us. It was extremely important for me to put all my cards on the table. Cindy could then assist me and together we could cover all the bases.

As we sat in her living room before a warm fire, I began to speak offhandedly, peeking at my notes.

"Cindy, I really respect Dr. Billings. He is dedicated and

believes in his work. He had some interesting comments at the conclusion of our session that I want to share with you. He first made it clear that not all of our problems derive from experiences in earlier lifetimes. Some may result from our current lifetimes and may have nothing to do with the past. However, regression analysis lends us the ability to go back and look at some troubling behaviors that seem to persist and bother us today, in our present life. In other words, we should analyze both past and present. Many times common issues can be identified that affect our relationships with others and have strengths of their own. These can evolve into phobias or extremely intense fears that have the power to dominate our emotions at any given time. Our prior lives grant us understanding and confidence to lead more successful, fulfilling current lives. Armed with this knowledge, we can address our phobias. In reality phobias are forms of anxiety, much like compulsive behaviors. Specific situations or obstacles that we encounter may precipitate great anxiety or abnormal fears. An example would be a person who might be afraid of cats or with an excessive fear of heights. Such fears may interrupt his daily life. Oftentimes, we recognize that these fears are irrational but feel powerless to change the behavior. The gripping desire to avoid these feared elements or situations serves to reinforce the behavior and does not help us learn to control or overcome the fear beneath. Most of these phobias are products of our childhood, and usually develop in adolescence or shortly after. Dr. Billings believes that the phobia I am encountering may not specifically be agoraphobia but rather another form of social phobia. Based upon his initial assessment of the taped recording, he is strongly convinced that the answer rests in my past lives. He told me that he will review the tape again to determine whether his original assumption is valid. In the meantime, he asked me to try to face rather than avoid such fearful situations. He also recommended that I meditate more frequently. He wants me to learn relaxation techniques that I can utilize as I need to and to remain calm at all cost."

Cindy listened intently to everything I related about Dr. Billings, then inquired. "Adam, did Dr. Billings mention anything about a support group?"

"Yes, he suggested that a support group may prove beneficial. He suggested one that includes desensitization therapy, behavior modification, and cognitive shifting. He offered to help me find an appropriate one. When the time is right."

"Were there any other recommendations?" she asked.

"He told me to refrain from using any over-the-counter drugs or alcohol—just the medications he prescribes. He wants me to make sure I get enough rest, eat a balanced diet, and exercise at least fifteen minutes every day, if possible. He feels that, in time, with the proper 'baby-step' techniques, I *can* overcome this phobia."

"That seems like very good, common-sense advice, Adam."

"I agree Cindy. As for treatment, once he is able to diagnose and verify my specific phobia, he intends to potentially add medication and supports maybe a natural remedy, such as kava kava. He assures me that many of his patients have been successful with self-hypnosis, which he may teach me in an effort to overcome my phobia. My public-speaking issue, he feels, is a symptom of a deeper problem. He reminded me that not all individuals have difficulty dealing with past life issues or traumas, no matter how painful, or how much they may have suffered. The reason is obvious. We are each unique individuals."

"Makes sense," said Cindy.

"Dr. Billings reminded me that people usually act in one of two ways: They keep the same behaviors and employ the same attitudes they owned in a previous life or, because of the trauma involved, go in an entirely opposite direction. So many factors need to be considered to interpret the information accurately. The ultimate goal of the therapy is to right the wrongs, to eliminate suffering, to improve the overall quality of life. That's his goal—and mine as well."

I continued. "Finally, Dr. Billings reiterated that reincarnation could be a major contributing factor. A previous incident in one of my lives could be influencing me big-time. People are usually not aware of past lives. Only on occasion may emotional memories carry forward beyond any memory or intellectual understanding of the originating event. One theory is that we would be incapable of coping with such information. It is kind of like a déjà vu experience. He gave the following example. Imagine walking in a park and encountering a person who had tried to injure you in a previous life. If you didn't fully understand the circumstances, you might not act appropriately."

"Fascinating." Cindy replied.

After a long sip of water, I went on. "Dr. Billings emphasized that humans overwhelmingly want and need to be connected or linked to society. However, when an individual cannot fully understand and connect to himself, it makes connecting to society even more difficult. Improving our recall to include past life experiences helps formalize memory and facilitate understanding. This provides us with clarity regarding our unique history."

I finished my notes and peeked up. Cindy was smiling.

"Adam, you explained that so very well. You are impressive. I am getting very positive vibes. I can't help but feeling you're on the right track."

"Thanks, Cindy. Now—to the tape?"

"That would be perfect." She showed another broad smile.

"Would you mind if I get another glass of water? Dr. Billings told me to drink plenty."

"Not at all. Let me get you some. I, too, believe in the power of water. They say that water cleanses the body and rebalances the mind. It is also beneficial to live near water. Boy, how lucky are we with the Pacific Ocean nearby and Oregon's abundant rainfall!"

We laughed. As we sat and listened to the tape, I couldn't help but notice how intensely she focused on every word. At times she seemed mesmerized by the dialog. She even jotted down reminders to inquire about at the conclusion.

As the tape concluded, she looked over to me. "Adam, that was absolutely riveting. I am amazed by your responses to Dr. Billings' questions. It ... gives me goose bumps."

"Was it a constructive regression Cindy?"

"One of the most convincing regressions I have ever heard. I've probably heard at lease fifteen in graduate school and about five more since. We experience our own regressions differently. Some of us visualize details. Others feel or sense virtually all that is happening around them. Some people can experience several lifetimes whereas others may only experience one. Your ability to capture these details—it's exceptional. Age, names, apparel, footwear, features, surroundings, even mood—it's just so amazing. In my unprofessional opinion, I'd say this session was very successful and confirms that you have, in fact, lived before. Adam, you hit the ball out of the park. Now to the important question: What does all this mean?"

"It may carry significance and meaning for someone who believes in reincarnation, but I just can't come to grips with the concept. Maybe it's too New Age or something? I was raised strict Lutheran. I don't feel I have ever lived before. The idea of even considering this notion seems way out of bounds. Cindy—do you believe in reincarnation or past lives?"

"I do Adam, I do. Let me explain. First, reincarnation goes hand in hand with past life regression. I believe that people are born to many lives. They evolve and develop and learn many lessons which makes them wiser human beings. Death is not the end of our existence. It is merely a transition of our spirit within our eternal journey of birth, death, and rebirth. We always carry with us certain energies from life to life. When we are born again we are allotted a precise interval of time to complete our spiritual assignments in the new lifetime. It is common for people to finish lifetimes short of reaching their spiritual goals. However, it is believed we do have enough time, so we must not waste it. If we finish our lives on earth and don't complete our assignments, the uncompleted tasks will be assumed in later lifetimes, most likely in other roles. Our goal is to live lives of love and compassion and transform ourselves into loving spiritual beings. When this is finally achieved, there is no need for further reincarnation."

Enthusiastic now, she continued. "Karma is an important element and part of reincarnation. We all are given free will as we encounter situations here on the earth. We have the ability to bring love, hate, optimism, pessimism, fear, and even indifference to these situations. If we choose negative responses, the chances are we will encounter the same lessons again in this lifetime or in future ones. We each have a set of Akashic records which reveal our soul's deeds during all its lifetimes. These records, housed in the spirit world, chronicle every moment of time within our life experiences, and document our numerous efforts to purify our hearts and become one with God.

Adam, I have actually heard stories in graduate school

about people who have unusual birthmarks. Past life regression has effectively tied these marks to earlier lives when they were burned, mutilated, or marked in some manner. We must remember that people who suffer some kind of trauma such as near-death experience or abuse usually grow in some way, including spiritual growth."

She paused for a long moment, reflecting, and then went on. "I have read that people will often reincarnate with others from former lives. Other times people are placed together in lifetimes for certain periods of time simply to accomplish a specific goal. When that goal has been achieved, they part ways. In reality everything is predestined or happens for a reason. Everything."

"Can we really believe the information that a person divulges under hypnosis?"

"That's a valid question, Adam. Have you have ever heard of Bridey Murphy?"

I shook my head no.

"Well, a woman named Virginia Tighe from Colorado was hypnotized numerous times in the early fifties by one Morey Bernstein. When under hypnosis she spoke and sang in Irish and told Irish stories. She declared she was, in fact, Bridey Murphy, a woman born in 1798 and died in 1864. Bernstein's book about this unusual incident, *The Search for Bridey Murphy*, became a best-seller. However, a closer investigation revealed that no individual named Bridey Murphy had ever lived in Ireland. Further research located a Bridey Murphy in the state of Wisconsin. It was further discovered that this woman had actually lived across the street from Virginia Tighe when she was a child. This startling find put a solid damper on all claims about regression analysis. It appeared now that all such stories were simply childhood memories and not verification of past lives.

Adam, I know you are very serious about this and motivated to find the truth. As in any science or any endeavor, there is always the chance of misinterpretation and sometimes exploitation, often by careless or selfish people. Regression analysis has come a long way since the fifties, but I just wanted you to be aware and to keep an open mind. We must not only trust in the concept of regression analysis but believe that, as individuals, we are capable of eliciting information from the past.

You know, when you mentioned religion before it felt like a déjà vu experience. I went through the same thought process about six years ago. I researched it. You see, I am Catholic, but I don't always agree a hundred percent with the Church's doctrine. I've always felt that reincarnation was not only plausible but very right for me. As it turns out, research reveals that reincarnation was an integral part of the Catholic faith many years ago. Some of the earlier sectors of the Catholic Church believed in the concept of rebirth. Roman Emperor Constantine wanted to create a common belief system within the church and the Council of Nicaea was established. However, the belief in reincarnation was no longer included in the new doctrine. Even though some still believed in the concept, they were eventually crusaded against by none other than the popes and were forced to keep their views private. I believe that it was far, far more than a 'common doctrine' and offered views that Jesus Himself would subscribe to. With this omission, it now gave the church more control over individuals and reduced not only our personal accountability, but moreover our being in charge of our soul's progression. Don't several Bible verses speak of the return of John the Baptist in the person of Elias? I personally believe that reincarnation is in perfect harmony with church beliefs and that the restriction placed upon the original believers was simply a power play." This she stated with conviction.

I couldn't believe how informed Cindy was on so many subjects. I wanted to sympathize, but once again my scientific background resurfaced.

"I apologize, but I have this mind set that seems to only gravitate to black and white proof, I said. I don't want this to end up like Bridey Murphy. I need more proof of a prior existence than what I elicited under hypnosis. In my heart I want to believe it as if it is the gospel. My healing process depends on it! But ..."

"Adam, the word "gnosis" comes to mind. It is Greek and means *to know*. We receive the gift of gnosis through a spiritual connection to our source. This connection lends us insight, acceptance of our challenges, courage, and finally spiritual growth. Meditation and hypnotic past life regression are vehicles to this knowledge. I believe with all my heart that you are on your way to receiving this gift. But it will not be a gift until you yourself believe it."

"I want to believe, Cindy. I want to. You know, ever since you mentioned birthmarks a thought has been going through my mind."

"What are you thinking, Adam?"

I looked at her.

"If we are to be a team, don't hold anything back," she urged.

"Okay. Couldn't my own bloodline or genealogy provide me with candidates for who I might have been in previous lifetimes? Couldn't the symptoms of my regression and past lives match my genealogy? Maybe this would yield an exact match."

"You certainly are a hardliner when it comes to authenticity and proof. I guess that's the scientist in you. I applaud you, Adam. Actually, I, for one, have never considered the link between reincarnation and genealogy. And that's really an interesting thought. Just where would you get a family genealogy?"

"Two weeks ago my Uncle Tom, my Dad's brother, brought over a copy of our family genealogy. I guess this is why I am linking it to my own case. He has been working on it for many years dating back to the eighties. He's traced back on my father's side to around 1545. He is still working on my maternal side and has already worked back to 1766, but he's currently stuck there. He gave us a copy. The supporting documents provide incredible detail—the kind of 'proof' that is right up my alley."

We nodded and laughed.

"You know Adam, this would satisfy your thirst for greater substantiation. It sounds interesting. I love the idea. Maybe your family tree would reveal ancestors who had the same issue. Talk about divine timing. Let's give it a shot. See where it takes us."

Before we knew it three hours had passed. Cindy ordered the pizza and we relaxed. I finally asked her if she was part Italian. She smiled when I explained the rationale behind my question. No, she wasn't, but she did love Italian food. Besides, she was much too tired to do any cooking.

After we ate, the talk turned to her. Cindy was slated to submit her first article within a month. Whatever she would write about, I knew that she was more than qualified. She had impressed me with not only her vast knowledge of the topics, but moreover her broad-mindedness and her ability to recognize and respect my perspective of pure science. It was a night of very interesting conversation. Most importantly, I got to know Cindy much better. I gained a whole new level of respect for her. As I readied to leave, we confirmed that at our next meeting we would delve into an in-depth analysis of my family tree.

My next appointment with Dr. Billings was scheduled for the upcoming week. He had promised to discuss his review of my regression and determine whether medication and a support group would be part of my treatment plan. I was looking forward to the meeting. I couldn't wait to tell him about my work with Cindy.

As we said good-bye, Cindy surprised me by giving me a hug.

"We are a pretty good team," she said, looking up into my eyes. "I have always felt I had a purpose in life. Facilitating projects like this and helping people makes me feel good. I know we are on the right track. You're an impressive guy, Adam. Thanks for coming. Please drive carefully—it's pelting rain out there. I'll see you in a week."

As I made my way to I-5 and then north toward Portland, I never felt so good. I was beginning to think, to hope— now almost desperately, that Cindy's interest in me and my bizarre case were not solely professional in nature. I didn't know if it was the regression analysis, the reincarnation or simply the thought of her, but something was telling me to go ... go ... go with the flow.

Chapter Five

S tudying one's own family genealogy can be quite an extensive undertaking. America, the land of the free and the home of the brave, has been referred to as a melting pot. People from all around the world have left their countries of origin to immigrate to America, seeking the right to the American ideals of life, liberty, and the pursuit of happiness. For most Americans, a study of family lineage may start in America but, after receding only a few generations, backtrack it's way to virtually any and all countries around the globe.

Uncle Tom had always been intrigued with history, and naturally curious about our own family history. Years ago, he had initiated his investigation into our family history, and was sparing no time or effort in his quest to unearth our ancestors. His goal was to trace the entire family lineage and compile as many supporting documents as he could muster. He wished to gain insight, to better understand each family member, to preserve each precious life story. He wanted to really "get to know" those individuals of previous generations, to uncover the stories that wove the fabric of our family's tapestry. Where did they live? What did they do? What were their hopes, passions, and dreams?

Since my uncle worked in the medical field, he was particularly interested in uncovering our family's health history. His search included determining causes of deaths or diseases more prevalent in the family. He wondered if cancer, diabetes, asthma, heart disease or maybe mental disorders could be traced in our family. His quest involved a variety of sources in his search for answers. He searched through birth records, death records, marital records, newspaper articles, deeds, name changes, church records, military records, probate records, petitions, shipping manifests, and naturalization records. He corresponded with cemeteries and libraries and reviewed U.S. census records. Some of the information came to him in different languages and required translation into English. Along the way, he was fortunate to find other distant relatives in our family embarked on similar studies. Teaming up and sharing information made his job far less cumbersome. In many cases, collaboration allowed him to pick up a trail where it had previously appeared to end. He specifically told me that he likened the study to piecing together a huge jig-saw puzzle, the pieces of which were scattered and hidden all around the world.

My mother, a family historian in her own right, told me that years ago people almost always married those in their own geographic vicinity. If a man did not own a horse, chances were good that he would marry one of the locals, someone within walking distance of his home. With the advent of new modes of travel like the ship and the train, the opportunity to meet a greater number of suitors increased significantly. Until that time explorers or sailors alone had the prospect of meeting women in distant locations. I remember Mom once exclaiming, "Thank God your father had a car when he was in college!"

In all, Uncle Tom's patient and tenacious search yielded a lengthy pedigree chart complete with records and unique stories supported by letters and documents. Meticulously he had documented the stories shared by distant relatives, noting when, where and from whom he had heard them. He actively searched for supporting documents, hoping to find a letter, newspaper article, or legal documents such as a formal notice—for collaboration on the stories.

My own newfound interest in our family history was not overlooked by my parents.

"What's behind all the questions and interest lately?" Mom put it to me casually at dinner one evening.

I decided to level with them. I related the events of the past few weeks, starting with my trip to Maryland and ending with my session with Dr. Billings. Mom and Dad were very understanding and reassured me they would help in any way they could. I suspect that they had always feared I was having some odd difficulty, but had decided it better not to interfere.

I told them about Cindy and how kind and supportive she had been over the past few weeks, and that Cindy planned to be in town the following weekend. They both looked forward to meeting her and asked me to be sure to invite her for dinner. I promised I would extend the offer.

The next week found me spending evening hours poring through the stacks of genealogy information Uncle Tom had gathered on my father's side, which had the most comprehensive information. My intention was to sift through all of the documents and separate them into logical categories pertinent to my analysis before Cindy and I would meet. We would use our time together as efficiently and as productively as possible. If Cindy and I could get through the paternal side of my family this week, we could finish the whole project by the end of the next. Since my paternal side was the most lengthy, I decided to start there.

I was extremely motivated and determined to discover the identity of this person and, more importantly, his or her significance for me. Based on my earlier regression with Dr. Billings, the compelling characteristics of this mystery person would be that of a female, possibly an outcast, possibly jailed, perhaps hanged. From the dialogue, this woman appeared to own a deep spiritual faith and strong convictions. Even though my regression pointed to a woman, I kept an open mind. The task seemed a daunting one, not unlike finding the proverbial needle in a haystack. However, with all this history at my fingertips, the clues were there. With diligence and scientific rigor, we could successfully discover the identity of this entity. Since I knew first hand that my grandparents showed hardly any of the characteristics, I decided to begin my search with my great-grandparents.

Thursday brought my next appointment with Dr. Billings. He was pleasantly surprised to hear about my progress to date and wanted to be kept appraised of the results. The genealogy aspect fascinated him. I told him about my diet, new exercise program, and how I was meditating each morning. I told him that giving up alcohol was so easy since I rarely drank any alcoholic beverages to begin with. As expected, he prescribed meds for relaxation and to alleviate my anxieties. I would start taking them immediately. He also had a support group lined up, slated for early November. He suggested we meet prior to the first group meeting, to discuss coping skills.

At approximately four on Saturday, Cindy arrived, carrying a bottle of wine as a host gift for my parents.

"What a thoughtful gesture, Cindy! How did you know this is one of my parents' favorite wines?" I inquired.

She simply smiled.

In the living room we enjoyed a leisurely chat, which surprised me. How natural and comfortable it was to relax and talk in my own home with a beautiful woman and my parents. We chatted for well over an hour. Cindy described her work as a psychologist, her job responsibilities, and her goals for the future. My parents thanked her repeatedly for all the assistance she had provided me.

"I've really enjoyed getting to know Adam these past few weeks," she said. "We really hit it off. I look forward to working with him." She smiled as she said it, then glanced from Dad, to Mom and finally locked eyes with me. I wasn't quite sure what she meant, but it sure sounded encouraging.

"Well, it has been a pleasure talking and getting to know you," Dad replied. "Hey—do you like steak?"

"Yes, I really do enjoy a good steak now and then," she said.

"Well, you are in for a treat. I bought some great tenderloin filets and consider myself a 'Master Griller.' Please excuse me while I go start the grill."

With that, both Mom and Dad got up to start dinner.

"It's Italian beef," I played.

"Adam—I do eat other kinds of foods too!" she said chuckling, shaking her head.

Dinner was as delightful as the conversation. Dad didn't exaggerate. He made what I consider to be the best steaks in town. When dinner was finished, my mother asked if we had any room left for dessert.

"I made a tiramisu. I'm part Italian too, you know," she added, eliciting laughter from everyone. "Adam, have you been spreading rumors about me?" Cindy asked in jest.

After dessert Cindy turned to my mother, "Let me help you clean everything up," she said.

"Guests are not permitted to clean up in our home, but thank you for offering," Mom grinned.

While Mom and Dad cleaned up, Cindy and I retreated to the family room and got to work.

"So, Adam—where do you want to start?"

"During my regression, it appeared that I may have also lived as my brother Michael. Let's start there. Honestly, this makes no sense! I may have been my brother in a previous life? Wow, and if you do believe in reincarnation, why would someone choose another life only to live a few, short weeks or months?" I inquired.

Cindy appeared to anticipate my question even before I finished.

"Timing plays a major part in reincarnation. Maybe the timing wasn't right. Maybe there was a lesson to be learned by the short life. Maybe your folks needed to learn a lesson and Michael fulfilled that need. We can't be sure of the reason. If you did reincarnate and you once were Michael, there has to be a specific cause. If that is the case, you have to ask yourself why you've been placed back in the exact same environment again. From what I have read and understand, I would be willing to venture a guess that this has something to do with your parents and their spiritual growth, or that the conditions for you were not right and had changed. Maybe this time around the circumstances are better for everyone to progress."

As I thought about this, it seemed to make sense. I was beginning to find the concept of reincarnation intriguing. Returning to the business at hand, Cindy and I began to review the genealogical documents on my father's side. The journey back began with Isabella Mayworm (1876-1955), my father's grandmother, and my great-grandfather Jacob Birk. I discovered that Isabelle Mayworm Birk was actually the second wife of Jacob Birk and the mother of Fredrick Birk, my dad's and Uncle Tom's father.

"Isabella, Uncle Tom's and my father's grandmother, lived with them when they were very young," I declared, paraphrasing the documents. "She died when Uncle Tom was eight. She loved to play Canasta with her grandsons. Isabella came from an educated and prominent family. Her father William was the city treasurer of Milwaukee, Wisconsin, around 1885. The Mayworm family of German Catholics had arrived in Philadelphia from Westfalia, Germany in the 1830s. William's father Christoff Mayworm migrated to Milwaukee around 1850. Uncle Tom still has very fond memories of his grandmother, although my father, even younger, has little recollection. To this day, Uncle Tom remembers Isabella reading the boys *Alice in Wonderland*. He also remembers her bringing him a special little present every time she went downtown to shop and tells me how amazing it was to live his younger years with a woman born the same year as Custer's Last Stand."

The documents were each fascinating. As a young adult, Isabella had lived in a convent, studying to become a nun. She was extremely devout, always carried a Bible and read from it daily, until the day she died. She was also a woman of few words. Before completing her training for the sisterhood, she had left the convent and married William Krause. Unfortunately, he died several years later, leaving her a childless widow at age thirty-four.

Around 1909 Isabella became acquainted with Jacob Birk, whose first wife Anna Schweiger (1876-1902) had committed suicide, leaving him a widower with four children. It is believed that she committed suicide because he refused to permit her to attend a church function one Sunday evening. Ironically, he married another deeply spiritual woman, Isabella, around 1909. The two eventually had four more children, with my grandfather Fredrick being the youngest. Even in her later years Isabella was devout, wearing a crucifix around her neck and carrying a Bible everywhere she went.

Jacob's family was strict Lutheran. His father Johann

had been one of the founders of St. Matthew's Lutheran Church in Milwaukee in the 1870s. On New Year's day in 1923, Hans, one of Jacob's sons from his first marriage, went outside in his undershirt to help a neighbor start his car. He cranked, but the stubborn old Ford wouldn't start. He worked up a sweat and caught pneumonia. Within a week he was dead. The pastor at St. Matthew's refused to allow Jacob to hold the funeral in the church, because Hans was not a member. From that day on, Jacob never again went to church. However, he did require his Catholic wife Isabella, to take his children to the Lutheran church and enroll them in the Lutheran school. From all accounts, it appears that the women in our family were quite outgoing and outspoken, but Isabella was the rare exception. She was never angry, and was apparently a very kind and peaceful woman. Fredrick, my dad's father, loved her dearly and took care of her until she passed in 1955.

I was fascinated by another story Uncle Tom shared regarding our German roots and how he had discovered our German relatives. After his and my dad's mother Marjorie died, Uncle Tom began working on the family genealogy. He came to regret that neither he nor his father Fredrick had taken time to ask his older relatives their recollections of family history, before they passed. He knew few details about his great-great-grandfather Johann Birk (1801-1871), who arrived in America in 1851. However, this was another dead end. Uncle Tom had lost the trail. He had no clues to determine where Johann had come from. Then, one

Sunday in October of 1979, Uncle Tom was in Bay City, Oregon, sifting through some of my grandmother's personal belongings. He came upon a family Bible. As he paged through, a piece of paper fluttered to the floor. Retrieving it, he recognized his mother Marjorie's handwriting. The paper was old, yellowed, tattered, but legible.

Apparently, Marjorie had sat down with my great grandmother, Isabella some thirty years before and interviewed her about the Birk family. One member she listed was Elias Birk (1833-1886), simply stating "Elias Birk, born 1833, brother, from Trossingen, Germany." Since Uncle Tom already knew that Johann Birk (1830-1907) had been born in 1830, he assumed that Elias was his younger brother. After a search he found Elias' death certificate in Milwaukee, Wisconsin, and from it was able to confirm that Elias had indeed been born in Trossingen. Fortunately, Uncle Tom speaks and writes fluent German. Knowing that Johann had been a founder of St. Matthew's Evangelical Lutheran Church in Milwaukee, he wrote a letter in German and included all the facts he had been able to uncover regarding Johann. He sent the letter off blindly, simply addressing it to "Trossingen Evangelische Kirche" in Trossingen, Germany.

Imagine his surprise one spring day in 1980 when he came home to spy a sizeable package from Germany on his kitchen table. He opened it carefully and inside he found what became known as "the genealogical mother-lode." A document written in German by a member of the Lutheran Church in Trossingen, it confirmed Elias' and Johann's relationship and documented the Birk family history all the way back to 1545.

All the accompanying documentation amazed Uncle Tom. In addition to facts, the respondent had sent anecdotes and vignettes regarding the family in the little mountain village of Bad Wurtemburg, West Germany. The Birk family had owned an inn called *Zur Lamme* or *The Lamb's Inn*. During the occupation by Napoleon's troops in 1803, Johann's grandfather—yes, another Johann—was the innkeeper. French officers commandeered the inn as their residence and took a liking to Johann's wife Ursula. As they were drinking and discussing their evil thoughts, Johann's young son overheard them planning to assault his mother. He told his father, who quietly took his family out the back door to relatives in nearby Rottweil. Realizing the family's escape, the French soldiers grew enraged. They destroyed all the furniture, smashed all the windows, and stole everything of value. They then set fire to the Inn, and the soldiers actively searched for the family. Fortunately, the Birks remained safely hidden and were never found.

Next, Cindy and I considered eighteen additional women who were part of the genealogy and who seemed to have the best chance of being my candidate. But though their stories proved very interesting, they did not describe the woman we sought. One by one we were able to eliminate the women due to a variety of factors such as age, background, or any number of other aspects. Only two of the women, Elizabeth Ritter (1829-1890) and Elizabeth Ripple (1855-1897)—had been known to be loners.

Other less likely candidates lacked information sufficient enough to urge us to consider them. Also, I noted that specifics regarding women in the family were not always fully documented. Many family items such as census, will, and marriage certificates did not include maiden names. Back in that time a women's life was seemingly not important enough to include in the public record. Birth records for women were not consistently recorded. Rarely was there a female death record to confirm her existence and mark even her minor place in history.

The remaining individuals Ursula Pfister, Appolonia Sponnhagen, Theresia Hersedy, and Elizabeth Hoelz gave me little to go on in the historical record. I wondered, had these women, too, been isolates? I couldn't help but recall how much this "loner" trait had been a part of my personality for as long as I could remember.

At eleven we decided to call it quits. After this careful review, I felt we had exhausted the most probable possibilities on my father's half of the pedigree chart. We had systematically eliminated each female for one reason or another. Also, Dad's side of the family had provided the most information in terms of names and documents. In fact, the pages traced all the way back to 1545. The last genealogy documentation revealed the Birk family paying taxes in 1545. The tax had been imposed in an effort to raise funds to create an army to fight the Turks. To have carefully traced and reviewed the histories and anecdotes of eighty-six of my ancestors was an oddly fulfilling exercise. But, I was still at a loss and not any closer to finding the mystery person. The analysis of my paternal side was complete, but it had led us to a dead end. However, we still had my mother's family genealogy to review. We remained optimistic. With careful digging, we would find the answers we sought.

Cindy mentioned that she would be traveling in two weeks and unavailable for a week. Last summer she had signed up to attend a phobia seminar at Yale University at the end of October. The seminar itself was only a day and a half long, but she would take time to visit the Boston area, something she had always wanted to do. She had always felt an affinity for the colonial times and wanted to experience some of our country's historical past.

Too, Cindy had sensed my frustration. "Adam," she declared, "we are making great progress. Although we haven't come up with the answers that we are looking for yet, don't let it get you down. I believe we are making progress and are getting closer to solving the mystery of your past. You are making great strides with Dr. Billings. We'll sort through the rest of the this, piece by piece, until we get to the bottom. If we stay focused, we'll get the break we need. I feel strongly about this. I know in my heart that this is true. We just need to believe. We must pray about it. And all this information about your family—hey, it's not just interesting but truly enlightening at the same time. I find it great fun trying to understand and assess your ancestors. The family members we have traced have proven to be people of strong convictions. Their viewpoints and decisions made under their trying circumstances, at their times in history, reveal very solid characters."

I nodded. "Thanks," I said. "I know we're making progress, just by virtue of getting through all this documentation." I conceded. "However, I was hoping for some substantiation by now?"

Cindy smiled, "I understand, Adam. I do. We will, soon, I promise. Have faith."

I looked at her and felt a flush of emotion. "You are really incredible, Cindy," I said then. Always upbeat no matter what the odds. Always positive. Always helpful. I don't know how I can ever repay you. You are ... probably the kindest person I've ever met."

She took me in. "That's kind of you. Very kind. But you know, Adam, when I was a little girl our family did not have money. Once we could not afford a new chair my mother badly wanted. Well, Mom taught me a very important lesson. She saved for four months to get her favorite chair reupholstered. The chair turned out beautiful. She was so proud of it. Shortly after, I was playing and accidently spilled a few drops of ink right in the middle of the new chair's cushion. Mom did not fly off the handle. She knew it was an accident. As for me, I felt terrible. But she simply got a needle and thread out and stitched a beautiful flower right over the ink mark. That day I learned anger does not help. We need to ask God for help and direct our energies to find solutions and fix the problems. I am so grateful to Mom for this valuable lesson. I guess this is why I enjoy helping people—whoever and whenever I can."

She smiled again in recollection. She too seemed moved. Then she took me in once again. "Adam, last Wednesday I found out that my associate at work, Jacquelyn, will not be able to attend the Yale seminar. We had been planning this trip for a long time. She is really disappointed. Her husband will be having surgery a few days before. She needs to be available. I have just had a most fascinating thought. By any chance do you have any vacation time left this year? Would you consider coming along? I'd be willing to bet you could easily re-book her reservations. Yale has a great science department. You could spend some time there. We could even continue our work on the trip. How's that for an offer?"

I stood by, nearly numb. This had taken me by surprise. "Wow, that would be ... great," I said. "But I would have to check with Dr. Gibbons. I do believe I have at least a week. I'll check Monday. I'll email you."

"Great. Just a thought."

It was late and Cindy had a long drive back to Corvallis.

She patted my arm. "Thanks for a wonderful evening. And Adam, please do thank your parents again for the wonderful dinner. I really enjoyed meeting them. I'll see you next Saturday at 5:00 p.m. in Corvallis?"

I nodded. "I'll get a head start on my mother's side. Hey, your optimism is contagious. Now I'm looking forward to sifting through all the documentation."

I walked her out to her car.

"Drive carefully, Cindy."

Impulsively I reached out and hugged her closely. My gesture came as a total surprise. Gauging from her glance, Cindy was as surprised as I.

Chapter Six

On Monday morning I confirmed that I had plenty of vacation time and I received approval from Dr. Gibbons. He seemed quite pleased when I told him about my plan to accompany Cindy to New England for her Conference and some site-seeing. Cindy sent an email inviting me to meet her parents the following Saturday in Corvallis. She suggested we meet them for dinner and finish up our work at her condo after. Our goal would be to get through all the remaining genealogy information on Mom's side. Then on the trip we could assess where we stood and plan the next step. The timing seemed perfect. My next appointment with Dr. Billings and the support group would be a few days after our return. Everything seemed to be falling right into place.

On a spectacularly clear autumn day, I made my way to Corvallis. The sky was a brilliant blue. There was no rain in sight. I wanted to make a fine impression on Cindy's parents. The more I thought about meeting them, the more anxious I became. And then I thought about Cindy. Always she had brought out the best in me. Immediately I felt a renewed sense of confidence. Somehow she would ease my nerves and break all the tension. We were scheduled to meet at the Big River Restaurant and Bar in downtown Corvallis. Cindy assured me the restaurant featured a wide variety of cuisine.

The four of us met in the lobby. Cindy's dad was a tall, distinguished-looking man with grayish hair and glasses. Her mother was the spitting image of Cindy. Some might have thought they were sisters. I could see where Cindy had gotten her appealing smile and laid-back nature. Like Cindy, her parents were extremely mellow as well. As I had anticipated, Cindy took pains to make the meeting comfortable for me. Over a scrumptious dinner, Cindy laid out the details of our upcoming trip. Fortunately, she had put many of the reservations in her name, so I was able to stay at the same hotels, now completely booked. We would be departing this coming Thursday and come home the following Wednesday. We would fly to Boston and drive to New Haven for the conference at Yale. After, we would drive back to Boston to take the trolley tour, then would end our trip with a few days in Salem.

When the check came, I picked up the tab. Although Cindy's dad protested, I could tell they were appreciative. As we said goodbye, Cindy's father pulled me aside. "Adam, thank you. It was very generous of you. And it's a distinct pleasure to meet you. Please do us a favor. Watch out for Cindy. Take care of her on this trip. We always worry so much."

"Mr. Parsons, I give you my word. I will do everything in my power to make sure she is safe and has a wonderful time."

He shook my hand. "Thanks, Adam, I knew you would. Have a wonderful trip."

I was surprised when Cindy's mother gave me a hug.

Cindy's parents had picked her up, so it would be convenient for me to drive her home. On the way we chatted about the work ahead of us. As we drove, I couldn't help but think about how amazing Cindy was. She was so kind, smart, and so very considerate. Spending a week of vacation with her would be incredible.

Soon back to work at Cindy's kitchen table, I handed her a pedigree chart for my mom's side of the family, as I had done with my dad's family tree. This way she could again logically follow along.

I had some exciting news to share to share with her. "Uncle Tom had placed a request for information in some national journals and periodicals about a year ago. A few months back Uncle Tom had been contacted by a distant relative, Ruth Anderson, which happens quite frequently during genealogical research. Ruth was the great-granddaughter of Almon Church (1836-1895), the brother of Aaron Church (1840-1917), so she was almost the same generation as my grandmother Marjorie June Birk (1919-1979) but a few years younger. She and Uncle Tom had both hit roadblocks at the generation of Joseph Church (1809-1898). They knew his wife had been Mary Beede (1811-1885) and knew that they had come from Vermont. Previous to that, they had been unable find anything about the family.

One evening Ruth called Uncle Tom. In an excited tone, she informed him that she had found someone in New England who had the missing piece of the puzzle. She told him that the Church family name was an adopted one, that our real name in that lineage was *Hogg*. Pleased to share the information, Ruth then sent Uncle Tom all the documentation which had enabled them to work back a few more generations. The Church/Hogg information led to the discovery of Joseph Church's parents, Alexander Hogg Church (1758-1849) and Patience Dumby (1766-1861). This newfound information opened the way to even earlier Hogg generations.

Within a short time, Uncle Tom sent Ruth a copy of the death certificate of Patience Dumby. He hoped she would be successful researching the lineage. Up to this point Patience Dumby had also been a dead end. One day Ruth mentioned to her ninety-year-old neighbor, a retired grammar-school teacher, the issue regarding Patience. The neighbor asked for the document—a death certificate written in the flourished handwriting of the day and was inscribed "Patience Dumby." Immediately the neighbor remarked, "It's not Dumby, it's Quimby!" When Ruth again looked at the name, she agreed it certainly could be. The Q looked so much like a D? Last week, Ruth confirmed that indeed it was Patience Quimby. She also has learned that the surnames Quimby and Quinby were often transposed because of the stylish handwriting of the 19th century. Ruth is currently researching this further. She and Uncle Tom are hopeful that this new breakthrough on the style of script will provide more ancestral information very soon."

"Wow!" Cindy replied. "That is an amazing story. You have to be a detective with a watchmaker's patience as well as a great deal of luck to get so far. Kudos to that penmanship teacher for breaking the code!"

"I guess that's true Cindy," I agreed with a smile.

A matter of luck and sheer coincidence? I then I told Cindy how Uncle Tom had learned about Burgess Rice (1850-1912) the father of my maternal great-grandmother (Blanche Rice) and my great-great-grandfather. "Back in the 1980s Uncle Tom had hit a similar wall regarding Burgess. What little he knew he had learned from my great-grandmother Blanche. Uncle Tom had determined that Burgess had been born in England, and had immigrated to America around 1850. After homesteading in Wenatchee, Washington, Burgess had settled in the Pacific Northwest. A steamboat captain on the Columbia River, he had sailed the Pacific along the west coast. He had also lived in Seattle (where Blanche was born), Garibaldi, Oregon, and even San Francisco. He had moved from San Francisco only two months before the famous earthquake of 1906. Uncle Tom had heard rumors that Burgess had had four wives and four families, but this he couldn't confirm. Then one day Uncle Tom mentioned Burgess to Blanche's brother, Burgess Rice, Jr., nicknamed Uncle Doz. Oddly, Uncle Doz replied, "Burgess had come west from Muskegon, Michigan." Uncle Doz then related a most interesting story.

One summer day in 1925 Uncle Doz was working in his motorcycle shop on Alder Street in Portland, Oregon. Across the street was a barber shop where he had always had his hair cut. On this particular day, a stranger walked into the barber shop, and asked for a haircut. As the barber began cutting the stranger's hair, he sensed a certain familiarity with this head of hair. Suddenly, something struck him.

After finishing the haircut, he asked the customer, "Please wait here two minutes?"

He ran across the street and beckoned Doz to join him at the barber shop. Doz came back with the barber to join the other in the barber shop.

The barber declared, "I've been cutting hair for 35 years and I know all of my customers' heads." Turning to the stranger, he said, "From your head shape, and the texture and color of your hair, you could be this man's brother!"

"That's impossible," said the man, "I just got here from Michigan. I've never been to Washington before in my life."

Doz then replied, "I was born here. The only states I have been to are California and Washington."

The two men stared at each other.

"Well, sir, then who is your father?" asked Doz.

"A guy named Burgess Rice." declared the stranger. "That's why I came out here. I heard that he had moved west years ago."

Doz nearly fell over. The two men began to share information. Indeed, they were, in fact, half-brothers. This half-brother, Albert Wolfiaul Rice, had been born in Muskegon, Michigan in 1870. He was some thirty years older than Uncle Doz.

After hearing this story, Uncle Tom immediately verified it through the 1870 census records from Muskegon, Michigan. There they were listed: Burgess, his wife Phoebe, and his family. Uncle Tom sent for the marriage certificate. When it arrived, it contained all the pertinent information about Burgess and his mother and father. His father, Robert, had been born in Frindsbury, England, outside London. An inquiry to the Royal Historical Society in London soon produced the marriage certificate of Robert and Phoebe Rice. The rest, as they say, is history. The Rice family long before, had come from Sherwood Forest in Lincolnshire, England.

So Cindy, that is how an observant barber in 1915 helped unravel an entire line of family history," I summed.

"Wow Adam, like another old saying goes—Only your hairdresser knows for sure!"

We laughed.

I had more information to share regarding the women of the Church family. "Martha Malissa Church (1868-1960) was the first white woman born in Long Beach, Washington. Martha was the oldest living daughter and, per custom, helped to raise all her younger brothers and sisters. On August 4, 1888, she married the earlier mentioned Burgess Rice, an immigrant steamship captain, in Astoria, Oregon, who had come from England as a baby in 1850. Forty-two years later, in 1892, my great-grandmother, Blanche Rice, was born to them in Seattle. Shortly after, the family homesteaded near Wenatchee, Washington. Life was difficult. Blanche shared many stories of her childhood with Uncle Tom. In the 'wild west,' encounters with Indian tribes was commonplace. It was not uncommon for Indians to ride up and steal clothes off their wash line. Medical and dental care was virtually unavailable. It could be months before a traveling doctor or dentist came through town. At one point, a suffering Martha was finally able to be treated by an itinerant dentist. On examination, he noted that many of her teeth were abscessed and rotted. Many had to be pulled. Now keep in mind, this was before the age of dental anesthesia. That same day Burgess came home to find Martha recuperating in bed. He demanded that she get up and make him dinner. Obedient to her husband, she tried to do so, but in the process collapsed and almost bled to death.

Blanche had told my uncle another frightening story. One day, when she was approximately two years old, she was sitting on the front porch, calmly feeding bread and milk to a rattlesnake. Her mother Martha came out of the house, sized up the situation, and slowly grabbed an axe (which was always handy). With one swift blow she cut off the snake's head.

Martha had a younger sister Agnes Martin. Around 1898, Martha's family moved from the farm to the Oregon coast, close to Agnes. A year later, Flora Martin was born. Flora was Malissa's niece and Blanche's cousin. Over the years the two cousins Blanche and Flora remained great friends and visited each other frequently.

In 1961, Uncle Tom had the chance to meet Aunt Flora, then living in Spokane, Washington. Marge and Fred Birk (Marge was Blanche's daughter) took two of their three sons, Tom and Rick, on their first trip to the west coast. They stopped for the night in Spokane. What a treat it was for the two young boys to meet Flora and her husband James Spence, then a spry ninety-four years old. In 1882 James had run away from home at an early age to become a cowboy. Now almost seventy years later, he had stored in his garage his prized possessions from those cowboy days—his saddle, knife, and bedroll among other memorabilia. All evening he entertained the family with tales of his glory days on the range from Wyoming and Montana to Texas and Arizona.

Sixteen years later, in 1977, Blanche learned that Flora, now a widow, was on her deathbed in Spokane. She flew to Spokane to see her for one last time. When she arrived, Flora called her into her room.

"Did ... you ever feel there was something special between us?" Flora asked Blanche.

"Absolutely. Yes, we were always quite close." Blanche said.

"We're more than close," Flora corrected. "We're half-sisters. When your mother Martha was dying, she called me into her room and told me. I've kept the secret all these years and never told you Blanche, but I think it important for you to know."

At this, they both laughed heartily and rejoiced in their sisterly bond.

"So it seems that Burgess did not always dock his ship in the home port while living on the Oregon coast!" I remarked to Cindy.

Cindy giggled.

After a pause I began again. "Pierre Napoleon Bonaparte Primeau (1864-1924) was born in Chateauguay, Quebec. Uncle Tom never knew much about the family in Quebec until one day in 2003, out of the blue, the granddaughter of Napoleon's sister called him. Uncle Tom had placed a notice in the *French-Canadian Historical Society Quarterly* in 1980. Relatives had recently found it by indexing. Ninon Biron, the granddaughter, was eager to be in touch with her newfound relative. Within days she sent Uncle Tom a packet containing the entire family history as well as some photographs. When they arrived, Uncle Tom perused the photos, and he almost fell off his chair. One image of Napoleon looks remarkably *identical* to my father, yet four generations and various ethnic roots separated the two."

I showed the photo to Cindy, along with one of my dad at precisely the same age. Cindy, who had just recently met my father, gasped and couldn't believe the resemblance.

"Napoleon had immigrated to America in 1888. He settled in Escanaba, Michigan, very much a French-influenced town. He must have had both money and the entrepreneurial spirit, because within twenty years he owned a hotel, a cigar store, a liquor store, several copper mines, and a lumber mill. His son Lawrence, born in 1895, liked to party. As the story goes, Lawrence, while growing up, had an extra key to the liquor store and often hosted his young buddies for a night of revelry at Napoleon's expense. Lawrence also learned the lumber trade, in which he was employed as a scaler. Drafted in World War I, he was sent out west to Vancouver, Washington to work the forests for the army. There in 1917 he met Blanche Rice at a dance. They married and after the war moved back to Escanaba, Michigan. It was difficult time for Blanche in terms of customs and language. The cultured French community was far different from her own upbringing in pioneer America. Additionally, Lawrence, now a railroad man, had a great affection for liquor far beyond the norm.

When Marjorie was born in 1919, Blanche had a very difficult childbirth. As she remained hospitalized for two weeks, her Primeau in-laws took the infant to St. Anne's Catholic Church and had her baptized Catholic. However, they did not tell Blanche until later. Blanche always deeply resented how this had been done without her knowledge or sanction. Phyllis, a second daughter, was born in 1921. Lawrence loved both his daughters, but Phyllis was the apple of his eye. The girls grew up in a fairly wealthy family. Blanche did not need to work and she grew extremely close to her mother-in-law Laura Salva Primeau (1845-1911). The Primeau men were typically French. They partied and frequented the seedy side of town, as was considered part of the culture. Laura grew more than irritated at their behavior and waste of money. Each time Napoleon came home to sleep his stupor off, she emptied his wallet and pockets and hid the cash. The next day when he couldn't remember what had happened to his money, she would chastise him and tell him to go look for it in the red-light district! When Napoleon died, Laura had saved enough money to buy herself a brand new house."

"One smart woman," Cindy slipped in. I couldn't help but smile.

"In 1929 Blanche's sister Ruby contracted spinal

meningitis. She lived in San Francisco. Since Blanche's husband Lawrence was a railroad man, his family had free train passes anywhere and anytime. In order to aid her sister, Blanche traveled by train out to San Francisco. She took Phyllis with her and left Marjorie in the care of Laura and Lawrence. While there, Phyllis contracted spinal meningitis, the same deadly disease that afflicted Ruby. Blanche and Phyllis returned to Escanaba, but within a week little Phyllis was dead. Great-grandma Blanche once told Uncle Tom, "If you haven't lost a child, it's impossible to understand the impact that such an event has on your life. Some people are strong enough to survive it. Others only make believe."

From that time on, Lawrence was given to even more dangerous binges. He would come home and break all the furniture. Other times, he would vanish for a week, and then return as sweet as pie. It destroyed the marriage, but one can only imagine the pain of losing a child. Blanche became bitter with God and sought answers by delving into alternative religions. One of these included spiritualism, which her mother Martha Malissa had practiced and which had been very fashionable in the 1920s. In 1936 Blanche separated from Lawrence and took Marjorie to Scappoose, Oregon for a year. She returned to Michigan one last time, but finally divorced Lawrence in 1939. It was a rare, courageous act for a woman in those days, especially considering the ongoing depression and the comforts in life she and her daughters had enjoyed. Lawrence never attended Marjorie's wedding, some ten years later, and knew little of her first son, my Uncle John. Lawrence eventually died as a hit-and-run victim in Los Angeles in 1945.

Blanche's daughter Marjorie also fostered a keen interest in spiritualism. She was an extremely bright woman with a great attention to detail. She used these qualities to publish a novel, a true-life account of her search, *Opening The Door To Spiritual Knowledge*. The book was far ahead of its time in 1977. Meanwhile, Blanche had lived a long, hard life, and always carried in her heart the pain of losing Phyllis. When Marjorie died of cancer in 1979, Blanche was once again devastated. Experiencing the death of her two daughters exactly fifty years apart was certainly her cross to bear, which she did uncomplainingly, until her own passing in 1994, at the age of a hundred and one.

One little-known member of our family is Sarah Francis Shaver (1847-1910). Her parents, Martha Kellum (born 1827) and John Shaver (born 1819), were married in 1846 in Keokuk, Iowa, on the mighty Mississippi River. In 1853, the family decided to head west to Oregon, home of some of the Shaver relatives. On the way her mother Martha either contracted cholera or was bitten by a snake and died. Having lost her mother en route, Sarah was eventually taken in by relatives in Oregon. She eventually married Aaron Church in 1864 in Portland, Oregon. Though her husband was a devout Protestant whose ancestors had been New England Puritans, one account tells of her exceptional interest in spiritualism and her extraordinary ability to hear disembodied voices. Could this could have been the result of the early trauma in her life?"

Uncle Tom's photo of her reflected the sheer weariness of her life. I showed the picture to Cindy. Uncle Tom said he often wondered what her life had been like without her mother and who, in fact, had raised her?

"Uncle Tom also told me just how he had discovered yet another branch of our New England family. Blanche Rice, Uncle Tom's maternal grandmother, lived with Tom from 1987 to 1993. One would think a centenarian would be feeble and senile, but such was not the case. Blanche was blessed with an incredible memory. In one instance, when her deceased husband's nephew Chuck visited her in 1990, he brought a friend named Shirley whom he had dated some fifty years earlier. On introductions, Blanche piped up, "Oh, I remember you. We met at a picnic at the Rose Garden in Portland in the summer of 1941." Both looked at each other in disbelief. Shirley confirmed the recollection. With this living encyclopedia in his house, Uncle Tom was very blessed to have access to so many years of family history and stories.

Blanche once related how, when she was a young girl living on a homestead near Wenatchee, Washington, her great-grandfather, Joseph Church (1809-1898) had lived with the family from 1894 until his death in 1898. While there was little to do on the farm but work and chat, one of Blanche's duties was to feed Joseph bread and warm milk. He had long since lost all his teeth. Even as a child, she listened well, and could recount many episodes in Joseph's early life back in Vermont and his trek across the Oregon Trail in 1846."

With this last story related, I was now back in the year 1766 where Uncle Tom was currently stuck with Patience Quimby. That was all there was. The track back into the dimmer mists of history had stopped. I turned to Cindy. She shrugged and then remarked, "Adam, I think you would agree, we haven't yet found our smoking gun. However, I don't know if you've noticed, but five successive generations had an unusually deep interest in spiritualism. Marjorie Primeau, Blanche Rice, Martha Malissa Church, Sarah Francis Shaver and Martha Kellum—each showed a keen interest. This in itself is telling and may be a step in our direction." She looked at me. "Adam, have you ever heard of the term 'metaphysics'?"

"I have. But I can't tell you what it means."

"It's a branch of philosophy. Its central branch is called ontology. Ontology is the study of all the different things in this world and their relationships to one another. This type of analysis lets us better understand ideas like time and space and life and what may explain their existence. It seems to me Adam, that you and I are gradually bridging the historical gap between science and philosophy. This is a very good thing. Basically, we are letting the cards fall as they may but at the same time considering variables, both scientific as well as philosophical. I feel that, as unlikely as it may seem, this last spiritualism link may prove far more important than we think. We just need to meditate, and pray, and give it time."

Having carefully reviewed these documents related to over five dozen entities on my mother's side, I had a newfound appreciation for my own personal history. But we were no closer to solving the mystery. Cindy and I were fascinated by the stories from an historical perspective, but we could not perceive their purpose. Maybe the spiritualist link that Cindy had made note of did have significance? We just didn't yet know. Where to go from here? One thing Cindy was right about: We needed to pray.

Chapter Seven

If you have never been to the Northeast in autumn you have missed one of nature's most wonderful gifts. The sheer beauty of the foliage with its painted leaves combined with all the fragrance and crispness hanging in the air create an ambiance amazing to behold.

Cindy and I arrived at Boston Logan on Thursday night at 5:30 p.m., right on schedule. The lengthy flight, fortunately, had been non-stop. We retrieved our luggage and our rental car. We intended to drive directly to New Haven, Connecticut this evening, home of Yale University and the site of the phobia seminar. It had been very rainy in Boston, and it did not appear to be letting up. As we began our journey on the I-90 Turnpike, neither of us could get used to paying money at the toll booths which seemed to appear all too often. The scheduled two-and-a-half-hour drive would extend an hour longer due to the heavy downpour of rain that hampered visibility. I kept reassuring Cindy not to worry. Hey, we were from Oregon. Both of us boasted years of experience dealing with a wet climate. We pushed on through the downpour, thankful for having thought to buy sandwiches and drinks at the airport. We ate as we drove, and hoped not to stop until we reached our destination.

The lights of New Haven were a welcome sight. We exited on Front Street, turned on College, and eventually came to George Street, site of the New Haven Hotel. Cindy had thought this would be a great place to stay as it was situated at the one end of Yale's campus. I dropped Cindy and the luggage off in the lobby and parked the car in the garage across the street. We secured our rooms, Cindy on the fifth floor and me a floor below on the fourth. We would be here for only two nights, as we would leave Saturday afternoon right after the football game. I would leisurely stroll and survey the campus on Friday and for three hours on Saturday morning while Cindy attended her final workshop. Cindy and I agreed to meet in the lobby at 7:30 for breakfast. She intended to leave right from breakfast for the seminar. It was to be held only six short blocks north on campus. We would meet again at 5:30 in the lobby after the seminar concluded for the day. We took the elevator to the fourth floor and I bid goodnight to Cindy. She looked exhausted, but, as usual, didn't complain.

The rooms were spacious and well-decorated. I was glad to have a king-size bed. I took a quick shower, watched a few minutes of news, and drifted off. I didn't realize how exhausting travel can be. The 6:30 wake-up call startled me. I rose, readied myself for the day and soon was downstairs. Cindy was only a couple minutes behind me. Already I had secured a table in the hotel restaurant. Cindy smiled and nodded as she spotted me and made her way over. She looked beautiful as ever, in a powder-blue dress. Over her left arm she carried her purse and a camelhair coat. In her right hand she clasped her shoulder bag with her laptop.

"Good morning Adam, did you sleep well?" she inquired.

"I did. Thank you. How about you?"

"Just great. And now I am ready for a wonderful day. Adam, I've looked forward to this seminar for a long time.

The keynote speaker is Doctor Keller. He is from Harvard and has an incredible background in anxiety disorders. I was extremely fortunate to have gotten into the seminar. Oh, before I forget, here's a campus map. I highlighted some places you may want to see, but they are just suggestions. Enjoy yourself. That red dot there is the science department. I am sorry you'll be alone today, but as I said, I'll be back here no later than 5:30. We can have a nice dinner together."

"No problem at all Cindy, I'll be fine. I look forward to exploring the campus. Thanks for the map."

After breakfast, Cindy left for the seminar. I lingered at the table a bit longer enjoying another glass of juice as I planned my day. The map was ideal and included all kinds of information. I knew we would be in a hurry after the football game tomorrow and with the anticipated crowds, I decided to fill up the gasoline tank before I started my campus exploration. I re-parked the car, and strolled easily up York Street on foot. It was a gorgeous day. Just like in Oregon, after a terrible downpour and vicious winds, the next day would so often provide sun and beauty. Today was no different. The campus was gorgeous, decked out with autumn colors sprinkled throughout the trees. At Chapel Street, I observed the famous sculpture garden and the art gallery. From there, I walked across to the Old Campus. It was inspiring to peer up at buildings which have been on the Yale campus for yes, centuries. The brickwork was exquisite, the high steeples breathtaking. Buildings like Dwight Hall and Vanderbilt had been frequented by many of their most esteemed alumni, an

America's Who's Who. I visited the Sterling Law School on Wall Street, followed by stops at the Sterling and Mud Libraries. This architecture was truly amazing, the sheer volume of books incredible.

At the Yale Bookstore, which was next on my agenda, I found a few souvenirs for my parents and Uncle Tom. Cindy wanted a Yale mug. I was pleased to find a glass one with a pewter Yale insignia. I also bought her a Yale t-shirt I thought she should enjoy. I had lunch at a popular deli, at an outside table amid the hustle and bustle of the college crowd. Although I had been out of school for only four years, I could still relate to each and every one of these students. I understood the stress and anxiety that was part of this college life, especially at a school like Yale, with the highest academic standards. I sat and people-watched, and began to relax. I started to think about all those people in my life who had been so concerned about me lately. Cindy? Dr. Gibbons? Mom and Dad? Uncle Tom and Dr. Billings? All were here for me. I felt blessed, very blessed. Yes, I must do everything in my power to resolve this issue. I won't let all these good people down.

After lunch I strode by the School of Management to the Class of 1954 Chemistry Research building and its adjacent labs. Since Yale is an open campus, I was able to duck in and listen to a lecture for about half an hour. By coincidence, the lecture was on genetic testing. I was awed by not only the size of the science buildings but the number of lab facilities on campus. My own chemistry background seemed paltry in comparison to this awe-inspiring environment. After the lecture, the instructor, who happened to be the department chair, took note of me. We started to chat. I was impressed that with his busy schedule he was willing to take the time to talk to a complete outsider and make him feel welcome. He seemed fascinated with my position with Cures and some of the projects I was working on. He gave me his card. I should call him, he said, if he could assist me in any way. I thanked him for his time and he wished me well in my future projects.

It was now nearly 3:30, so I turned around and started back across campus. On the way I observed the Yale Repertory Theatre with its red doors. When I reached the bookstore and the Grove City Cemetery, I knew I was over halfway back. And yes, it seemed quite odd to me that the graveyard was located directly in the middle of a college campus.

I wondered how Cindy's day had gone. I was looking forward to her company and a great dinner. As I made a sharp turn, I beheld an unusual structure. There stood a rather large monument adorned with what appeared to be pieces of quartzite stone of different shapes and sizes flanking two pillars. Across the top, bold letters made an unusual declaration: 'THE DEAD SHALL BE RAISED.' I stood momentarily mesmerized and fascinated not only by the irregular design of the monument but the energy it seemed to project.

When I arrived back at the hotel, I sat in the lobby and waited for Cindy. Somehow I could not get the words from the monument out of my head. 'THE DEAD SHALL BE RAISED' continued to echo from my head. At once I spied Karen, the hotel concierge. I stepped over and asked if she knew anything about the memorial and its unique message. It seemed strange to me that a prestigious Ivy League School would house a cemetery smack dab in the middle of campus. Karen, a retired high-school history teacher, who had lived in the area her whole life and knew its history quite well, filled me in. "Yale is a place of immense knowledge and history. The cemetery is perfectly situated because of its historical link to the city. For many years New Haven residents had buried their dead in the New Haven Green. Because the site was becoming overcrowded and rather messy, a new cemetery was created shortly after 1800. It would now be called The Grove Street Cemetery. In 1845, a wall of brownstone was built around most of the grounds, along with a small section of iron fence along Grove Street. Through the years there has been much controversy about the wall. It is now a national historic landmark and run by a private corporation. I think it's one of the oldest incorporated cemeteries in the United States. At the southern end of the cemetery is the entrance gate that you refer to. This structure exhibits the Egyptian Revival theme, a type of architecture very popular in the early 1800s. A professor once told me that the theme has something to do with Osiris, the Egyptian god of the afterlife."

I inquired further, "That saying, THE DEAD SHALL BE RAISED, I've seen those specific words somewhere before, but I can't put my finger on it."

"Yes, you probably have. They come from the Bible. They are in St. Paul's first letter to the Corinthians. I believe it reads, *'In a moment, in the twinkling of an eye, at the last trumpet, for the trumpet will sound, and the dead will be raised imperishable, and we will be changed.'* And if you have a musical background, you'll recognize them too. These same words form the foundation of a majestic aria from Handel's *Messiah.*"

"Wow," I said. After talking to Karen, I far better understood the significance of not only the structure but also its historical place on campus. It certainly allowed for a peaceful, tranquil atmosphere. I thanked Karen for her time and applauded her intellect. My time with her was very rewarding.

Just before 5:30 Cindy returned. She declared that she had a superb day. We went to our rooms to freshen up for a few minutes and met downstairs around six. We walked the few blocks over to Temple Street, looking for a restaurant. Still undecided, we ambled up Temple towards the Omni New Haven Hotel looking for that perfect spot. We finally settled on a quaint, little restaurant that specialized, of course, in Italian. A laughing Cindy promised that we would try other cuisines on the trip as well. We enjoyed a nice dinner. Under the circumstances and because of my medication, Cindy didn't broach the subject of wine. Over dinner she told me about her seminar. "Dr. Keller is a dynamic speaker. He really cares about his work. He discussed state-of-the-art techniques for anxiety disorders. Do you know that people with anxiety disorders are actually using Internet chat rooms and joining self-help groups? However, extreme caution must be used with the Net. You can never be sure of the source of the information. He emphasized that there is no substitute for a certified, trained professional. He strongly advised that any and all medications, including caffeine and cold medications, must be avoided unless approved by a physician. Again he advised that a support group like family members or good friends is an extremely important help to recovery."

"It's funny, Cindy. Just a few hours ago I was thinking again about how lucky I am to have so many special people in my life. I really appreciate you."

"Thanks, Adam. But you see, you are making the best of your circumstances because you have a positive attitude. There's no substitute for that."

Dinner was scrumptious. We talked until after nine, then took a slow walk home. I escorted Cindy to her room and said goodnight. We would meet again in the lobby, suitcases packed, at 7:15 in the morning. I couldn't believe how quickly these last two days had flown by. Although I had made good use of my free time, I had enjoyed my moments with Cindy the most. After tomorrow's two and-a-half-hour wrap-up session the seminar would be over. We would be together the rest of the trip.

After breakfast Cindy walked to her seminar. I checked us out and loaded the car. I took a short walk, then sat in the hotel lobby and read the morning paper. By late morning Cindy was back. Immediately, we drove to the Yale Bowl, the sight of Yale's football game against Columbia. Cindy told me she had always wanted to attend an Ivy League school. She loved to watch football ever since her brother had been a star high-school quarterback. She was an avid Oregon State fan, but wanted to experience the ambiance of Ivy League football.

"You see Adam—I have my own bucket list at the ripe old age of twenty-seven," she exclaimed.

We shared a laugh.

I, too, liked football games and had been to a good number of games at Linfield, a school with a winning tradition and a stellar gridiron history. The games were exciting and usually high-scoring. Upon arriving, we parked the car and walked across a large grassy span toward a series of tents. Along the way we encountered tailgating students dressed in various costumes and painted faces. As we tailgated, we found that by virtue of purchasing a ticket, we were entitled to a hot dog and a soft drink. The fans were very jovial and made us feel welcome.

Entering the stadium, we encountered a huge inflated bulldog, Yale's mascot. It must have been at least twenty-five feet high. The Yale band was decked out in its Yale blue uniforms and played a lively rendition of *Louie, Louie*. But by no means was the game a sellout. We learned that, with the exception of the Harvard game, this generally was the case. We found our seats and thoroughly enjoyed the game.

Yale ended up winning in the late stages by a score of 31-28.

We left just after Yale took the lead with roughly four minutes to go to get a head start on the traffic. We were out of the stadium and on the freeway within fifteen minutes, heading back to Boston. This time we took a different route, east on Highway 95 across a section of Rhode Island near Providence. The drive was filled with gorgeous scenery, compliments of the beautiful autumn colors. We arrived in Quincy, Massachusetts, where we had reservations at the Marriott Boston Quincy Hotel. Before check-in, we stopped to attend a five o'clock mass at the local Catholic church, St. John the Baptist. Being a few minutes late we caught the service in progress. The white church with a trio of handsome steeples poised high above its contrasting blue doors was striking. The service was different than that of my Lutheran church in Tualatin, but gave me an uplifting feeling. Cindy was a paragon of piety and devotion. I was grateful for the time to reflect in the house of the Lord. I had so much to be thankful for.

We checked in and shared dinner in the hotel restaurant. Afterwards, we confirmed our reservations on the Red Beantown Trolley. Tomorrow we would be spending the entire day on a tour of Boston. Cindy could hardly wait. Seeing Boston, she would now be able to cross one more major item off her bucket list. For me, I, too, loved history and could hardly contain my excitement. But the thought of seeing it first hand with Cindy made it all the more an adventure.

Chapter Eight

It was another stunning morning as we stood with the others in front of the hotel waiting for the trolley bus to arrive. As it was scheduled to be an all-day tour of Boston, we dressed very smartly, with coats, hats and rain gear. We wanted to be prepared for the temperamental Boston weather.

The bus pulled in. We stepped up, paid our fee, and found seats. After we had all grown comfortable, Charlie, our assigned tour guide, proceeded to emphasize "rules" of the day. He made it sound as if we were a bunch of kids going to camp for the first time. Immediately this created an atmosphere of solidarity and camaraderie from everyone on the trolley. I sensed that he was a well-seasoned tour guide, and this was his intention all along. Before long, he had us all roaring with laughter as he tried to convince us of the "treacherous perils" we would most likely incur on our trip through Boston and especially at Boston Harbor. Emphatically he explained that if we were to "survive" this trip, we needed to band together!

The ride into Boston took about forty-five minutes, as we had to make one more stop at another hotel, to pick up a couple visiting from Indiana. Charlie explained that, once in Boston, we could exit the trolley at sixteen possible locations to further explore Boston on foot. He distributed maps and pointed out the stops marked one through sixteen, and the descriptions of the sites at each stop. He emphasized that we all mark the central stop, number six. This he said was the most important stop. This was where the bus would pick us up at the end of the day for the return trip to our hotel.

Our tickets entitled us to jump on and off any of the Red Beantown Trolleys the entire day. We could get off at a specific stop, see the local sites and shop for souvenirs at our leisure. We could re-board any trolley and continue to the next stop or stay on the trolley and forego any side trips, if we chose. The tour actually began at the central point, the sixth stop on the map.

Of course I had assumed we would get off the trolley and investigate each of the stops in a chronological order. However, Cindy had a better idea given to her by a relative. Her aunt who had taken the tour a year before, suggested a different strategy. After explaining her aunt's logic, we decided that the suggestion made a lot of sense. The strategy was to get an overview of all the sites on the tour, prior to getting off at any of the stops. This would provide a good overview of the city and a better perception of where each site was in relation to the others. Then we could come back and visit the sites of greater interest.

We stuck to our plan, and stayed on the trolley for the entire ride around the city, noting the particular sites from the bus. After the overview of the city, we chose Stop Number One, the excursion cruise along the Boston harbor to start our adventure. We had heard that on occasion large crowds gather to make the return cruise, causing a bottleneck at the Charlestown Navy Yard. However, this was more apt to happen at the end of the day, which could cause people to be stuck for hours. To optimize our time and not take any chances, we decided to take the cruise early in the day.

As we boarded our boat, the *James J. Doherty*, we noticed it had three decks. On such a clear, beautiful day, we moved up to the top level to enjoy an unobstructed view. This turned out to be a good decision as it also provided a much better opportunity to take pictures. The cruise would take about forty minutes. After the boat was untied from the dock, the horn sounded, announcing it was time to disembark. Now we would see first-hand what we had heard and read about for years.

With a hand-held loudspeaker, our guide described important landmarks in the city's history. The most popular was the site of the famous Boston Tea Party. As our guide poignantly recounted, at this precise location, on the night of December 16, 1773, a group of angry patriots masquerading as Indians had boarded ships that had transported tea from England to America. In retaliation for the unfair taxes imposed by Britain, the enraged citizens had opened the containers and tossed the tea overboard into the Boston harbor.

Another highlight, the Old North Church, was another of Boston's most-noted landmarks. On the evening of April 18, 1775, Robert Newman had climbed to the top of the church steeple with two lanterns. He was charged with warning the town if the British, camped in Boston, were on their way to attack Lexington and Concord. A signal had been devised. If Newman held up only one lantern, the British attack was via a stretch of land connecting Boston to the mainland. If they arrived by ship, he would hold up both lanterns. Thus the famous quote was coined "One if by land and two if by sea." Viewing this signal, Paul Revere began his now-famous midnight ride throughout the night to alert the colonial militia, the famous Minutemen.

The Boston Light was another historical site. Built on Brewster Island in the harbor in the year 1716, it was America's first lighthouse. This lighthouse suffered considerable damage by both the British and the Americans in the Revolutionary War. It underwent an extensive rebuilding in 1783.

As we took in the sights and the sounds of the city, Cindy and I were fascinated. We could feel the history and culture more and more with each moment. It was incredible to believe that we were edging past the very spots where so many historical events had occurred. Cindy took a host of photos, the Boston skyline, the harbor, ships in the harbor, and the impressive buildings and architectural marvels, along the way. I did as well. We would make duplicates of our pictures and share with each other. We were pleased when the couple from Indiana graciously borrowed our camera and volunteered to take several pictures of Cindy and me together. Cindy was in her zone. "Adam," she gushed, "this is just incredible! To finally see the exact spots where all these famous events took place. I never dreamed it would be so beautiful!"

I smiled, "Awesome, right. And we've only seen the tip of the iceberg. Your bucket list is going to take a major hit today!"

She grinned and shook her head.

"Starboard you can now observe Bunker Hill," called the voice. We had looked forward to the Bunker Hill Monument and now it appeared, right on cue before our very eyes. It featured a 221 foot granite tower with an exhibit area. The Battle of Bunker Hill was fought on June 17, 1775. However, most of the combat actually took place on nearby Breed's Hill, where the monument stands. This monument marks the site of the first major battle in the Revolutionary War. "Don't fire until you see the whites of their eyes!" was the legendary order given by William Prescott, an American officer. His rationale was to give the under-equipped Americans a higher probability of success with their limited supply of ammunition.

As the boat approached port, we observed the *U.S.S. Constitution* in the distance. "Old Ironsides" as it was nicknamed, was large and majestic in its docked position, in contrast to extensive warfare it had endured. After going through naval security, Cindy and I toured the vessel, a real treat. She was in mint condition. Her construction and arsenal is vastly outdated by today's standards, of course, but it was amazing to consider the nerve and the fortitude of the brave men who manned her, especially in harm's way.

After we left the ship, Cindy and I walked over to Causeway Street to see the famous Boston Garden, home of the Celtics and the Bruins. Instead of crossing the Charles River via the Charlestown Bridge, we took another route suggested by a fellow-passenger on our boat. We entered a small park and went through a series of locks that brought us only blocks from the Garden, saving us oodles of valuable time. To our surprise, the Garden doors were open. We found it was Fan Appreciation Day, sponsored by the Bruins. This enabled us to see the entire arena. It was currently set up for hockey with ice covering the main floor. Much to our surprise, we were able to watch the Bruin's hockey practice from front row seats. Cindy's dad was an avid Celtic basketball fan. She made sure to take plenty of pictures of the world-championship banners and retired jerseys, from those incredibly successful teams, teams that adorned the ceiling.

Moving south, we came to Massachusetts General Hospital, then to Beacon Hill, where we viewed the huge estates on Mt. Vernon Street. Beacon Hill, originally developed at the end of the 18th century, is home to many wealthy Bostonians. The gas-lit lanterns and cobblestone surfaces enrich the quaint atmosphere of the streets. The highlight of Beacon Hill is without question the State House that had been built in 1795, which features a beautiful gold dome. The Beacon Hill district is considered a National Historic District.

The next trolley stop was the Boston Public Gardens. We jumped onto the trolley and traveled past John Hancock Hall to Copley Place, a luxurious shopping mall featuring over seventy-five high-end stores. Cindy didn't want to get off and browse. She knew our time constraints. I was relieved.

We continued on to Fenway Park, home of the Red Sox. From the street we viewed the Green Monster, the famous high fence in center field. My dad wanted a picture, so I obliged him. In front of the stadium, I noticed, stood a statue of one of the most famous Red Sock players, Ted Williams, befriending a boy. This provided another great picture.

Next we viewed Kenmore Square, a famous hub for buses, streetcars, and parties. Riding across the Charles River, we came to MIT and Cambridge University. Located directly on the Charles River, these two schools are both prominent institutions of higher learning. The trolley looped back across the Charles River and took us back to the Boston Public Gardens. Here we got off and found an outdoor cafe. We enjoyed a fine lunch and reviewed our day. It felt good to sit and relax for a while. We were ahead of schedule, so after lunch we spent a few hours in the Boston Public Gardens and the Boston Commons. The Gardens, created in 1837, featured meandering pathways to exotic imported trees and unique plant displays. The Boston Common situated right next door was created in 1634. It is the oldest park in America, occupying close to fifty acres. Here marks the spot where the British camped just before meeting the revolutionaries at Lexington and Concord. In the 1830s cattle grazed here and as late as 1817 there were public hangings in the Commons. We sat for a few moments and enjoyed music provided by local musicians who play for the community free of charge, although donations are always appreciated. It was a Sunday, so the park was filled with students, families, and visitors.

From the Commons, Cindy and I walked to the Old State House. Here the Declaration of Independence was read to the public from its balcony in the year 1776. Close by lies a circular path of cobblestones honoring the site of the Boston Massacre, where five revolutionaries died at the hands of British troops. We continued on to nearby Faneuil Hall, the birthplace of our country's first town meeting. Outcries against the British government erupted from this building, to include the well-known cry "No taxation without representation." I couldn't help but consider how brave these citizens must have been!

We boarded the trolley for the short ride to the theater district. In its early days, the popularity of plays dropped drastically due to the harsh Puritan stand against entertainment. Because of the Puritans extreme influence, the imposed ban lasted until 1792. The Puritans' had migrated to America in the 1620s because of religious intolerance in England. They felt civilization spoiled Europe. However, America had not been their first choice. They had gone to Holland about a decade before in their effort to avert English religious intolerance toward them. However, they became disappointed when their children began to speak Dutch and grow ingrained in Dutch culture. The Puritans felt they were losing their identity, so they came to the howling wilderness of America to cleanse their culture of such vices as drinking, gambling, swearing, and showy dress. They wanted to formally honor the Sabbath and felt that civil government should enforce public morality. To them, it was important that each person be seen as godly to become a member of their church. In essence, these Puritans were motivated to create a true kingdom of God, a pure religion. It was their destiny, they assumed, to transform the American wilderness into God's paradise on earth. For these reasons they closed the theaters. The district eventually became very popular again only around 1900. However, attendance fell once again, and considerably. By 1980 the district seemed on the verge of collapse. However, since that time the theater has actually made a strong comeback and the district once again thrives.

By this time, Cindy and I now felt we had sight-seen enough. We had used our time wisely and covered a great deal of Boston. We ambled the short distance to the Four Seasons Hotel, Stop Number Six, the final pickup point. Registered for the ride back to Quincy, we took seats in the lobby. It had been a memorable day. The sense of history in Boston is beyond description. The day's visual wisdom lent us a strong feeling and connection to our country's past. Just as the history of our country is the basis for its present framework and our society today, Boston made me realize even more that no one can progress without some understanding of his own beginnings. I was beginning to think in ways I had never thought before. Maybe Cindy was right. Things do in fact happen for a reason. At first glance this trip occurred 'by chance,' but could it be destiny or perhaps a part of my transformation? I had Cindy to thank for challenging me with this new concept and thought process.

After our ride back to the hotel and a leisurely dinner, we decided to make it an early night. We would depart no later than 6:30 a.m. Boston commuter traffic was notorious and we wanted to avoid it at all cost. Yes, tomorrow would provide another challenge as we would continue our look at New England's history. Now our quest would take us to another city with a storied past.

Tomorrow we would head north to Salem.

Chapter Nine

I met Cindy in the lobby at six sharp. Salem was situated about twenty miles north of Boston and because of the busy Monday morning traffic, we wanted to get a head start. We drove through Boston smoothly, with very few traffic issues and continued past Revere to Essex County. Passing Lynn and Peabody, we noticed the turnoff for Marblehead before finally arriving in Salem. When we arrived at 7:45 a.m., it was still dark and foggy. We passed a small "WELCOME TO SALEM" sign. Cindy was a bit surprised that the sign was relatively inconspicuous, given the town's storied past. "Salem will forever be remembered for the Witch Trials from the 1690s. Perhaps they are trying to tone it down a little," Cindy said.

Famished, we stopped downtown at the historic Hawthorne Hotel for breakfast. The hotel was named after one of the city's most illustrious sons, Nathaniel Hawthorne, an iconic nineteenth-century writer and former resident of Salem. The hotel was a majestic, seven-story structure located only blocks from the waterfront. Inside we found our way to Nathaniel's, one of two restaurants on site. Cindy mentioned that months ago she had attempted to secure a room at the hotel, but it was fully occupied. Fortunately, she had found an alternative local bed-and-breakfast, the Amelia Payson House, only blocks away. Luckily, she had booked both reservations in her name. If she hadn't, I would have been out of luck. Bookings for Halloween week are secured about a year in advance.

We enjoyed a leisurely breakfast both choosing the

continental breakfast, which was ample. Our waitress, very personable, told us about the upcoming festivities planned for the week. Since Salem is a tourist haven, the local businesses are more than eager to promote the city's activities that celebrate and embrace its past. She mentioned that Salem's police cars have the emblem of a witch on their side panels and additionally, the witch is also the mascot of the local high school, the Salem Witches. She recommended several of the local attractions. Since it was October 30th, the hotel was preparing a huge gala to be held tomorrow evening on Halloween. With this information, Cindy grew very excited and asked me if I would like to go. I agreed, and we purchased two of the last tickets available.

It was just past 9:30 a.m. when we finished breakfast. We drove up Washington Square north past the Salem Commons to Winter Street. There stood the Amelia Payson House, blue with white trim. Originally built in 1845 for Amelia and Edward Payson, the home featured Greek Revival architecture. The proprietors, Ada and Donald Roberts, were warm and welcoming. They quickly showed us to our rooms. Within thirty minutes we had unpacked and reconvened in the front parlor, eager and excited to begin exploring Salem.

Ada and Donald mentioned that we were only blocks from the Salem Witch Museum. We decided to walk to avoid parking issues. We had been warned that within hours, the city would be invaded by a sea of thousands who descend on the city every year to participate in and enjoy the Halloween activities. Already we could note a budding crowd on the streets. We felt fortunate as it only took about fifteen minutes to secure our Witch Museum tickets. Cindy and I joined a group of about twenty and were led into a dark room and seated on benches. On the floor in front of us was a lit red circle. Within this circle were additional concentric circles, listing some twenty names. The room was dark, but once my eyes adjusted, I could vaguely discern three dimensional scenes along the walls.

All at once I began to get dizzy. My heart started to pound. I began to sweat, profusely. In the dark, Cindy didn't notice my condition, which worsened. Just as the program was about to begin, I stood and asked to be excused. I whispered to Cindy that I would meet her outside. An attendant helped me out.

Outside, I sat and waited. After the show Cindy stepped out, concerned, but by now I was feeling much better, almost my usual self. "I don't know what happened. Cindy, I got light headed. It was very uncomfortable in there. With this fresh air, I feel much better."

"This is your first symptom of this nature since Maryland, right?" Cindy asked.

"Yes, that's right."

" What could have brought it on?" she continued.

"No idea. Maybe I ... just something I ate."

Cindy thought for a while, "Well, let's both keep a close eye on this," she said. "You know, Adam, you missed a great show. This production explained in depth everything about the witch trials. The costumes and the overview were professional and authentic. It was emotional. I wish you could have seen it. It gave me a whole new perspective for this period in history."

"Sorry," I replied and shrugged.

"Adam, back in 1692, witchcraft was a public offense under English law. The famous witchcraft accusations began when the village doctor diagnosed the young daughter of the local preacher, Reverend Paris, as bewitched. Soon a vengeful hysteria took over Salem as young girls called out the names of their alleged tormenters. The accused were tried, sentenced, and sent to jail. The final count was approximately two hundred people being jailed and twenty paying the ultimate price of execution. Several others also died in prison."

"Interesting how hysteria can spread, isn't it?" I remarked.

"Right. Would you come into the gift shop with me?" Cindy inquired.

"Absolutely, I do feel much better."

We spent about half an hour inside the gift shop purchasing some items for home. After, we returned to the Amelia Payson House to get the car. We would next explore the Pioneer Village, adjacent to a park on the outskirts of Salem.

Upon arrival, we noticed a trail leading beyond the village. We decided to follow the path which took us to a scenic hill and picnic area overlooking the sea. We took some spectacular photos and then returned. Back in the village, we were greeted by two women and a man in authentic

Puritan attire. With our camera they took pictures of Cindy and me with our heads and hands stuck through the holes of the wooden stocks. In the 1600s, this served as a form of public humiliation and punishment. They also posed for pictures, and we then started our tour in earnest. We came upon a three-acre village, a recreation of the Colonist's early settlements. With the extremely cold winters, warmth was a critical element to structure. Several dwellings of various sizes were featured. We saw small homes built partially into the side of hills, called dugouts. We observed wigwams, thatch-roofed cottages and larger wooden homes. Many of the homes were actually quarters for several families. Each featured a fireplace, the main site for cooking, with large hanging kettles and a nearby wood supply. Outside were vegetable gardens and a blacksmith shop displaying an array of tools utilized in the era. Cindy and I now had a much better understanding and a higher respect for the hardships these early settlers bore. It must have been difficult just to survive.

After our visit we drove back to downtown Salem and were pleased to find a parking spot and a quaint cafe where we enjoyed a light lunch. After lunch, we strolled amid the shops and boutiques. Cindy thought it would be great fun if we dressed in costume for the Gala Ball. We found a costume store, but its inventory was almost depleted. In fact, they only had a few women's and one man's costumes. What did fate provide? Cindy chose to go as a witch. Due to lack of options, I would attend the Gala Ball as a hangman.

Only a short walk down Essex Street brought us to the famous Witch House. This residence was the actual home of Jonathan Corwin, a judge during the trials. This two-story home is Salem's only structure with direct ties to the trials. Both Cindy and I were fascinated by its furnishings and the everyday household items. I felt mesmerized by the long, narrow table in the living room. For a moment I stared, wondering its purpose.

Back to the Amelia Payson House, we relaxed before dinner. We would dine at the Hawthorne Hotel this evening. Dinner tomorrow on Halloween would be out of the question with the Gala Ball in full swing.

Since the Hawthorne Hotel was easily walking distance from the Amelia Payson House, we decided to walk. Arriving right on time for our 6:00 p.m. reservation at the quaint Tavern Restaurant. The hotel was even more festive than it had been earlier this morning. The staff had done a remarkable job of decorating and transforming the decor. We were treated to an outstanding meal. Cindy had the fish and I chose the shrimp. We each decided to start our meal with a heaping bowl of clam chowder.

We had covered a lot of territory today. We were looking forward to exploring more of this fascinating city tomorrow and capping it all off at the Halloween Gala Ball at the hotel. Yes, it had been a full day. We were almost weary as we trudged the few blocks back to the Amelia Payson House. We looked forward to a good night's sleep.

The next thing I knew, I was awakened by a loud

buzzing. Seven a.m. had come all too quickly. This being our last day in Salem with a very full schedule ahead of us, I took extra time straightening up and getting my items in order. I finished getting ready then met Cindy downstairs for breakfast. Ada and Donald gave us more tips on what to expect today. Salem would be overrun by the huge crowds and their festive celebration.

By nine we were out the door and on our way to Pickering Wharf, the waterfront district fronting Salem harbor. There we browsed for over an hour in some impressive shops and boutiques already jam-packed with shoppers. One shopkeeper told us that Salem had a Wicca organization. He insisted that most people fail to understand that Wicca is a peaceful, modern creed, as opposed to witchcraft, which is ancient and not truly considered a religion. Wiccans he told us, seek lives of harmony.

By ten we were at the House of the Seven Gables, the original home of Captain John Turner. This spectacular home, built in 1668 was a handsome showplace. Alongside the home lay seaside flower gardens designed in 1909. Nearby was a lesser structure we could tour on our own. Surprisingly, we found that this dwelling was the actual boyhood home of Salem's famous author, Nathaniel Hawthorne. His original home had been moved to this location years earlier. It seemed a fitting permanent place to have this symbol of his boyhood home in such close proximity to the House of Seven Gables. It was Hawthorne's many visits here to the Turner-Ingersoll Mansion that was truly the inspiration for his 1851 novel of the same name, *The House of the Seven Gables*. The story features a curse placed on Hawthorne's own family by a person condemned to death during the witch trials. Folklore implies that only generations later, when a descendant of the victim married a niece of the Hawthorne's family, was the curse lifted. Allegedly, Hawthorne's own great-great grandfather, John Hathorne was a Puritan and the first of the family to emigrate from England. He became a magistrate and judge in Salem and was well known for his harsh sentences. He was, in fact, one of the judges who presided over the witch trials. As a young man in his twenties, Nathaniel Hawthorne was dismayed to make the discovery of his connection to Hathorne. To dissociate himself from his ancestor and his heartless acts, he added a "w" to his name, thereby changing it from Hathorne to Hawthorne. His good friend Herman Melville dedicated his equally famous novel, *Moby Dick*, to Hawthorne. Some say the famed 'W' carved into the sea by Ahab's ship does not symbolize a *whale*, but rather a *witch*, lending support to his good friend Hawthorne and is a poignant reminder of Hawthorne's decision.

Hawthorne, revered and admired even today in Salem, is considered a favorite son. His statute on Hawthorne Boulevard commemorates one of America's great writers. But Hawthorne was not always the town hero. His novel *The Scarlet Letter*, published in 1850, caused considerable chagrin in the religious community. In the novel's introduction, named *The Custom House*, Hawthorne painted the Puritans as sin-obsessed and intolerant. The story's ill-fated love affair between Hester Prynne and young Reverend Dimmesdale, producing the illegitimate, energetic, headstrong Pearl is evidence enough. As punishment for not publicly revealing her lover, Hester must wear a scarlet "A" to tell the world of her adultery. Throughout the story, Hawthorne demonstrates the kind, loving, and caring ways of Hester as opposed to the stern behavior demonstrated by the Puritans. After the novel's publication it took many years for Hawthorne to return back into the good graces of Salem.

"So, do you think that those who had fled to America due to religious intolerance become religiously intolerant?" I posed.

"Most certainly," Cindy replied. "You know what is also peculiar? Throughout history people's disagreements over their interpretations of God have resulted in many holy wars and deaths. That's not very holy. Isn't that just ironic?"

I nodded. After thinking about it, she was right.

We grabbed a sandwich at a local café, a late lunch. It felt good to sit after being on our feet most of the morning. Already it was approaching mid-afternoon. The Gala Ball would start at seven and end at midnight. We decided it would be a good idea to head back to the Payson House and catch a short nap. We had been on the go all day and wanted to be refreshed for the Costume Ball.

As the day had worn on, the crowds had increased in number. Ferries were running from Boston every other hour. Many partiers chose to park in Boston and make the forty-five minute voyage. The trains had added more cars and were bringing thousands more for a night of ghostly celebration in Salem. We noticed that most of the people arriving were already decked out in festive costumes. We drove home and parked the car for the night. We would go on foot the whole night, as would everyone else. Excitement and autumn crispness hung in the air. Already it was beginning to feel that this would be one incredible night to remember.

Chapter Ten

A slight knock came at my door, followed by a familiar whisper. Cindy said we needed to be off in about fifteen minutes. After a solid one-and-a-half-hour nap I felt invigorated. I slipped into my costume, feeling a little bit uncomfortable as I edged my way down the stairs to present myself to Ada and Donald. They grinned as they observed my hangman's attire. Moments later, a figure arrived in the parlor, dressed in all black and donning a high, steepled-like black hat. We all laughed.

After a few pictures I confessed, "Cindy, you are the best-looking witch I have ever seen!"

"Thanks Adam, I don't know if I look that great, but except for this—oops—hat, this outfit is mighty comfortable."

Ada and Donald told us to enjoy the festivities and to have a good time. To them, we must have resembled two kids trick-or-treating for the very first time. The Roberts had probably been through this too many times. But as we were leaving, I felt a tingle, a strong premonition that something extraordinary was about to happen. I didn't know how or why, just a feeling. After all, it was Halloween.

We walked down Winter Street and turned on to Washington Square Boulevard. There we observed hundreds of costumed figures standing, talking, shouting, screaming, and laughing. A trolley buzzed by packed with passengers in elaborate attire. It seemed like we were in the middle of an ant colony, and the ghostly city of Salem was the biggest hill. There were sites for storytelling, witch tours, fright night—even haunted ghost cruises on the harbor. As we neared the Hawthorne Hotel on Hawthorne Boulevard, we beheld a parade marching steadily down Derby Street. We continued past the statue of Nathaniel Hawthorne and found a less occupied perch to take in the parade for nearly a half hour. Figures filled the sidewalks at least ten deep for the celebration. People yelled, hooted and cheered as each float rolled by, seemingly better than the one before. The last display, showing a haunted house with a quintet of witches scowling out at the crowd, drew a huge, protracted round of applause.

Cindy was enjoying herself and became very animated. "Adam, this is amazing, simply amazing." This she said with a slight, playful cackle in her voice.

I laughed. I tried to elevate my mood to match her enjoyment, but I was certainly having a difficult time. My rope belt, supporting a noose, was beginning to cause some discomfort.

We went back up Hawthorne Boulevard to the Hawthorne Hotel. With the vast crowd at the door, it took more than ten minutes just to get in. Once inside, we were overwhelmed by the decorations. Since lunch yesterday, the transformation that had taken place was remarkable. They were absolutely amazing. Everyone was in costume. The theme for the evening was "Bedlam Behind Bars." Tables of food stood everywhere, lined with numerous hors d'oeuvres. Beer buckets sat in ice. There were several open bars. Cindy had a drink or two, but, with my medication and doctor's orders, I stuck to a sparkling water with lemon. One ballroom had a band. The other two had disk jockeys. Cindy wanted to dance and I reluctantly jumped in. It appeared she may have had a dance or musical background the way she seemed so comfortable as she moved. My own performance left something to be desired, and I was happy to be in costume and not recognizable. For the next few hours we danced, ate, drank, and toured. The hotel had Celebrity judges to determine Best Individual Costume, Best Group Costume, and Best Theme of the Ball. There was even a contest for the best room designed by a hotel staff department. The winners would take home cash prizes. Ada and Donald had said that it was highly unlikely for people to win with costumes that they had purchased. The best chance for success would come to those who had personally designed ones. The hotel staff intently searched out those unique outfits that stood out and best displayed the theme of the night. There were at least three photo stations. We took some crazy, bizarre shots, several with people we had just met.

At 11:30 p.m. the party was still going strong, but, the music and drinks would end at midnight. Cindy learned from a hotel employee of a candlelight vigil scheduled for midnight. It would start at the hotel and make its way down Hawthorne Boulevard, to Charter Street, and on to the Witch Trial Memorial. The memorial is a monument to each and every victim afflicted by the trials.

We decided to participate. Precisely at the stroke of midnight, Cindy and I along with roughly seventy other party-goers, still dressed in our costumes, convened outside the front door. We formed a loose line and were each given a lit candle safely supported inside a small lunch bag. At the front of the line was our leader James, the town historian. Next was Sarah, a story-teller, followed by Liz, winner of the best individual costume. Cindy and I were numbers four and five. It was an impressive sight as we began our trek down Hawthorne Boulevard. The onlookers cheered and hooted. Despite the still-huge crowd, everyone was extremely courteous and respectable, ceding our group the right-of-way as we marched over to Charter Street. We encountered the hustle and bustle of those hurrying to ferries, trains, and other modes of transportation in their efforts to leave town after a memorable day. We turned right and streamed down Charter Street. We were only about a block from the Memorial and James held up until the last of us had caught up. We then slowly walked the last block together, in unison. We huddled around James at the entrance to the Witch Memorial. He gave us a brief history and described the significance of the memorial.

"This Memorial, built in 1992 borders the Old Burying Point Cemetery, the place where Nathaniel Hawthorne's ancestor John Hathorne is buried. As you may know, Hathorne was one of the judges who presided over the trials. This is also right across the street from the site of the original Salem Meeting House, where many of the accused were interrogated. The Memorial is dedicated to all victims of this tragedy. It serves as a lasting tribute and reminder of the need for understanding, compassion, and tolerance."

After a moment of reflection, he continued. "I'd like to stress that this is a memorial, not the final resting place of the victims. The exact location of their remains is unknown. If you walk through the cemetery over there, you will notice that the graves face the opposite direction than do the markers in the Memorial. This is by intention and symbolic in design. This reminds the world how this community turned its back on the accused. You will also notice a single wall containing partial iron fencing. The fencing represents those being held in jail against their will. Many of the trees on this site are the black locust, a tree last to flower and first to lose its leaves. This in itself is a symbol of adversity and of the injustice of the trials. As we enter the Memorial, note the words cut into the stone of the doorsill. They are the words of protest from the victims, protests cut off in mid-sentence."

Now pointing to one inscription, James continued. "Here's an example: *'I AM INNOCE—.'* This is representative of the town ignoring their pleas of innocence. Inside the Memorial you will observe twenty stone benches, one for each victim. Each is inscribed with the name, date and means of execution. The benches are made of hand-hewn granite constructed in preciously the same manner as they would have been in 1692. Any questions? Okay, everyone let's go."

Again we lined up in single file, a procession that would enter the sacred grounds, and began. We came to the first stone bench in honor of the first person executed, Bridget Bishop, hanged June 10, 1692. Viewing the site, I grew queasy. Our group quickly moved to benches two and three.

There we found Sarah Good and Rebecca Nurse, both hanged July 19, 1692. As we approached the fourth bench, our group momentarily took pause. At once I felt a vibration—my cell phone. At first I fumbled the phone, then drew it out of my pocket. I was alarmed to discover that Uncle Tom was calling me at such a late hour. I immediately thought of my parents.

"Hello, Uncle Tom—is everything okay?" I inquired.

The voice seemed very excited and spoke very rapidly. "Everything is fine. I hope your trip is going well. By any chance, are you still in Salem?"

"Yes, we arrived yesterday and are still celebrating Halloween as I speak," I answered.

"Sorry to disturb you at such a late hour. I won't be long. I have some startling news to share with you."

"What is it?" I timidly inquired.

"Remember the woman from Washington I've been collaborating with regarding the genealogy? The one who discovered the correct spelling of 'Quimby'?"

"Ruth Anderson?"

"Right. Well, she faxed me some information a couple hours ago. You won't believe what I am about to tell you. Simply because of her neighbor recognizing that one letter, she now had the correct spelling of Patience's last name. Based on that information, Ruth was able to dig back four generations before Patience Quimby. Adam, you, me, all of us—we're direct descendants of Susannah Martin!"

I thought for a moment. "Who is Susannah Martin?" I inquired with a slight lump in my throat.

"Adam, she was one of the accused hanged in 1692. This is why I wanted to catch you while you were still in Salem."

I peered down. My eyes suddenly focused on Marker Number Four, almost directly below my knees. I stared down at the granite bench. All at once its engraved letters seemed to lift off the stone and hover before my eyes. The enlarged letters stared back at me!

SUSANNAH MARTIN
HANGED
JULY 19, 1692

I don't even remember responding to Uncle Tom that night. Immediately I grew flushed, light headed. Instantly, a conspicuous shiver migrated down my spine. The sweat came profusely. Then came an onslaught of chills, a numbness, leaving me unable to speak or even gather my thoughts. Suddenly, I was thrust back in time. A collage of images crowded into my brain permitting recall. I began to tremble. I was in a crowded courtroom, at a long table. Loud voices were erupting all around me, amid wild commotion. My mind rapidly flashed to another scene. I was on an old rickety wagon, pulled by horses. Then finally I stood before a boisterous crowd as they jeered, taunted, and humiliated me.

Just as suddenly, I came back to the present. As I looked up, costumed figures were murmuring all around me. Once again, I vacillated on the edge of time, of space. Now I was standing on a ladder tilted against the thick limb of a black locust. High above the crowd, I was subject to more slander and public humiliation from the onlookers. At once, something cut into my neck. I could hear the crowd chanting "Witch! Witch!" I fought, gasped for air, mumbled as best I could for the Lord's mercy. Then suddenly, I came back again. I caught a glimpse of a face—Cindy's face—unmasked in anguish. And then all turned as black as this night itself.

I woke in my bed at the Amelia Payson House. I had no idea how I had gotten there. I peeked over to spy Cindy, seated in a chair covered with a quilt. She was peering off, worried, tired.

"Hi," I whispered. "I guess I've done it to you again. Sorry."

"Adam—do you feel all right?" she asked with a look of deep concern. She then stood up and leaned over toward me.

"Tired. Really tired. But I guess I'm all right."

"Adam, do you have any idea what happened tonight?" Cindy inquired.

"I'm not really sure. It's ... all quite fuzzy." I replied.

"Well, you took a phone call from your Uncle Tom?—and you started acting very strange. I thought you might be having a seizure. Luckily there was a doctor in the group who immediately attended to you. He stayed with you until you were stabilized and he helped me get you back here."

"Where?"

She looked at me. "The Amelia Payson House," she said.

I looked around. Nothing seemed familiar.

"The doctor said that you would probably sleep for a few

hours but should be fine when you awoke. He gave me his number and asked me to call him when you are awake."

"I'm ... fine," I managed.

"While you were resting, I called Uncle Tom to let him know what happened. He explained to me your conversation regarding Susanna Martin. Did you know that Susannah Martin is a direct ancestor of those five women who show a flare for spiritualism. I assured your Uncle Tom that as soon as you were able to you would call home."

"Cindy, I have to tell you something. I peered around almost afraid to confide. I've ... been here before Cindy. As we made our way to the memorial I was having a lucid, déjà vu moment. Susanna Martin? I've never heard of her." As I spoke, I noticed my voice was raspy. "Who is she?"

"While you were with the doctor, I had a chance to talk to several locals, including the town historian, James, who was leading our group. Susannah (North) Martin was one of five executed on July 19, 1692. Ironically, you were just in front of her marker when you blacked out."

"I don't remember. Who is she?"

"Susannah was baptized a Puritan in Olney, England in 1621. In 1646 she married George Martin, a blacksmith by trade. In 1668 her father died. She and her sister Mary learned that his original will had been altered to leave almost everything to her stepmother. In 1669 Susannah was charged with witchcraft for the first time and required to post 100 pounds. Some say the property trial may have been a hidden motive for the charge. Apparently she was acquitted of this earlier witchcraft charge. Then in 1671, after her stepmother died, Susannah and her sister fought an endless legal battle over the estate. They appealed the case several times, but eventually lost the case along with their inheritance."

"And then?"

"On May 2, 1692 Susannah was arrested again on another charge of witchcraft. Incredibly, she was unsuspectingly served her warrant that ominous day by a longtime friend. Under examination she declared that, in her opinion, she felt the supposedly afflicted girls who had accused her were not bewitched. This enraged the star witness for the prosecution, the young Ann Putnam. It was also reported that Susannah disrespected the court. She spent the next two and a half months in jail, in deplorable conditions. The suffering and mental anguish she endured in jail was far beyond comprehension. Additionally, she was also subjected to harsh and cruel physical examinations.

On June 26, 1692, her trial began. Susannah entered a plea of not guilty. Testimony from the trial indicates that she considered herself a holy and God-fearing woman. Vehemently she denied all ties to witchcraft. Under pressure, the outspoken Susannah didn't know what to say to convince her accusers of her innocence. She declared what she believed to be true in her heart. Her responses were truthful and heartfelt. Some speculate that a theological debate ensued between the highly intelligent Susannah and the magistrates, which may have further angered the court. In the end, she was found guilty and sentenced to death."

"I'm beginning to put this together," I said.

Cindy continued. "On July 19, 1692 Susannah Martin along with Sarah Good, Rebecca Nurse, Sarah Wilde, and Elizabeth Howe were taken in horse-driven wagons to Gallows Hill. There the five were hanged. It is believed that their bodies were eventually pushed into nearby rock crevices and covered with dirt. It is reported that the relatives of Rebecca Nurse were able to retrieve her body and only she was given a proper Christian burial."

"Was the crime ever corrected?" I asked.

"Adam, it was. Within a year, a change of heart beset the Salem community. It was becoming ever more obvious that the victims had been wrongly accused. In late 1692 the Court of Oyer, charged with the responsibility of hearing the witchcraft cases, was disbanded. In 1693, when the Superior Court denied further use of spectral or supernatural evidence, the witch trials came to an end. The governor pardoned those imprisoned for witchcraft, and by 1694 witchcraft was no longer illegal. In time, Ann Putnam, one of the young accusers, repented her responsibility in the witch trials before the church. In the upcoming years the community even made restitution to some of the families and later adopted amendments absolving these relatives of further blame and embarrassment."

"That's good to know," I said.

"The victims of the trials were casualties of their time and place. Their small village was cut off from the world, in the middle of a frightening wilderness. Additionally, revenge may have played a role. As people would accuse others, a payback mentality spread like wildfire across the community. Adam, the people lost sight of God and acted against His will. This was in clear violation of the Ninth Commandment, *Thou shalt not bear false witness against thy neighbor.* Yes, slander does fall within the bounds of the Lord's command. In 1692, everyone knew that witchcraft was a serious civil offense yet some people of the time slandered their neighbors, accusing them of witchcraft. Was it possible the accusations were used to disguise the accusers own greed, jealousy, or pride? No doubt. The trials might never had occurred had townsfolk cared to look into their hearts and recall Jesus' words, 'Let him without sin cast the first stone.'"

I could only shake my head.

"Adam, this really bothers me because it shows a universal human failure. These victims suffered the ultimate penalty. No doubt Susannah's death involved anger, terror, and sadness. Her power was taken away as she feared for her life. Did she question God for allowing such injustice in the world that He has created? I have been reflecting on this. As humans, we were not created to suffer. However, we do suffer, starting with our first breath of life."

"Amen," I said.

"Yes, the fate of Susannah Martin affected us both deeply. Aren't we all part of a sinful, selfish world? It hurts terribly when we suffer and unfortunately, none of us is immune to suffering. When we suffer, God suffers. I sometimes wonder if perhaps God allows suffering, in order to cleanse the world of sinfulness. Who would better understand human suffering than God Himself? His son, Jesus, died for our sins and has risen out of this vale of tears. His resurrection gives us hope. Death is not an end but a beginning. Through His example we are born again to eternal life. It has been said that those who suffer for their principles enjoy a special place in God's kingdom."

Cindy was studying me. "Adam, do you remember your regression? When you were questioned by Dr. Billings, you referenced going from the wagon to the immensely peaceful feeling. Interestingly, I have read that just before a violent death, the soul vacates the body, allowing the individual to avoid the pain."

Cindy hesitated for just a moment, then looked me in the eye. "Adam, I believe what you believe—that earlier this evening you found your link and, yes, were viewing your own memorial. Somehow you and I ... we've been led here. Coincidence? There is no such thing. You've been touched and been given an immense gift, a chance to go back in time and witness the origin of your phobia here and now. A professor once told me that the stress hormones generated in an extremely fearful or dreadful situation, which in your case was giving that speech—equal those produced in facing death. I never imagined how spot-on that information would be. This newfound information will be extremely vital to your healing. You have been given a gift. You must use it wisely."

Cindy leaned over, and planted a soft kiss on my cheek. "Now try to get some rest," she whispered. "I'll call the doctor to give him an update. See you in the morning, early? We need to be to the airport by eleven."

I made a brief call to my folks and told them everything was fine. They were relieved. I slept well—so well that when I awoke I wasn't quite sure what of the previous evening had been fact or fiction. I showered, dressed, and packed. When leaving the room, I took pause to peer into the handsome antique mirror poised above the old dresser. As I glanced, the reflection of my appearance seemed slightly altered. Mirrors reflect the truth of our waking lives, but this mirror seemed to transmit ... something much deeper. The emotions and the feelings of my unconscious had been extracted from deep within my soul and forged into my expression. Was I viewing a different person? Or, was I now living in a slightly altered dimension?

On our way out of Salem, we stopped to purchase a dozen white roses. With Cindy at my side, I made a final visit to the Witches Trial Memorial and solemnly laid the flowers on Susannah's marker. We said a prayer for her, and for all souls so deeply affected by this tragedy. I asked God to grant them his love and mercy. I had been apprehensive about returning to the Memorial this morning, but with Cindy, I got through in flying colors. Afterwards, a great peace came over me.

As we began to exit Salem, at once a road sign fuzzily appeared, **YOU ARE LEAVING SALEM.**

"That says it all," I smiled.

"Says what?" Cindy asked.

"The sign."

"What sign?" She said.

I glanced at the rearview mirror, then slowed down. I craned my neck for a long moment, peered back. She was right!

As we traverse the rocky path of life, our journeys may be difficult to appreciate. Each life is a unique experience inviting us to participate and become active participants. But with our spiritual eye we can perceive goodness along the way. Life has adversity, yes, but, more importantly, what do we do with it? Do we recognize the blessings? Or do we constantly dwell on the negative and the bad? Do we need help along the way? We need to merely look for tell-tale signs. They are everywhere.

Yes, blessings are everywhere. If only we read them as such. For me, there have been tell-tale signs posted along the landscape of my life journey. From my phobia study to my befriending of Cindy, from my regression to my genealogy, from the prophetic words, 'THE DEAD SHALL BE RAISED' at Yale to the divine timing at the memorial in Salem, from the playful antique mirror at the Amelia Payson House to the improbable Salem departure sign, I have been fed a constant diet of blessings.

I realize that along with these blessings, a certain level of forgiveness will be required on my part, even though I am generations removed. Yes, now I must invert the hourglass and begin a life anew. I have limitations, but I am not a victim. As a Christian, I turn my cheek. I forgive. Thereby, I release all the negative emotion associated with this episode. Putting this long-lived trauma to rest heals not only my own physical being but my soul. I can heal and find peace. God had touched my heart and soul in His own special way. My return to Salem has been immensely rewarding. Cindy was right. Things do happen for a reason. The road to salvation is not always a direct route. Our Father has a special place in His kingdom for all those who were martyred. Those persecuted will now be released and will reap their just reward in God's heavenly kingdom. The fastest horse to heaven is through suffering.

Like Paul on the road to Damascus, I realized and heard a voice. I am a changed man. After ridding myself of hidden obstacles in my subconscious that barred my advancement, now unconditional love is possible. Unconditional love is a product of first loving ourselves, without judging oneself. I will rigorously pursue my own self-discovery regardless of my ancestral roots or tendencies. I now have a far deeper appreciation for history. For it was history that urged me to undergo my rebirth. What matters most is not the length of a genealogy, but more importantly, its width. The more traits that feed, the more experiences that nurture, the healthier our lives can become. This I know first hand, for the apple didn't—and doesn't—fall far from the tree.

Epilogue

I composed this story predicated on my own experiences, beliefs, and genealogy. At its conclusion I felt an enormous sense of peace. This being said, *Finding Adam Empowering Susan* not only provided this reward, but it actually took my emotional state a step further. How stunned was I to discover my own genealogical roots some sixteen years ago. Yes, I am, ten generations removed, a direct descendant of Susannah North Martin. My direct linkage connecting myself to Susannah is listed for you here.

Rick Birk (1951-Present)
Marjorie Birk (1919-1979)
Blanche Rice (1892-1994)
Martha Church (1868-1960)
Aaron Church (1840-1917)
Joseph Church (1809-1895)
Patience Quimby (1766- 1861)
Esther Hadley (1730-1793)
Joseph Hadley (1700-1758)
Jane Martin (1656-1704)
Susanna North Martin (1621-1692)

Based on this remarkable discovery, I can't help but consider my uneasiness while gathering and concluding my research last year in Salem. As I laid the roses on Susannah's memorial, I prayed for her and for all those souls so deeply involved in this tragedy. This simple tribute symbolized their innocence, reverence, humility, and that the truth would forever set them free. I can now conclude with certainty that the world is united historically much more than I could ever have imagined. Not only was my link to Susanna Martin an eye-opener, but a further unlikely twist left me more than perplexed.

Recent inquiry reveals not only that Alexander (Hogg) Church married Abigail Atwood, the great-granddaughter of Susannah Martin in 1754, but that Hogg himself had his own ancestral association to the witch trials. He was the great-grandson of Jane Hogg, accused of witchcraft in 1657 but never convicted. Amazingly, Jane lived in Amesbury, and was a neighbor of Susannah Martin. Consequently, each side of their family was tied in their own way to this tragedy. Might we even conclude that, much like Nathaniel Hawthorne, in order to finally distance himself, and his family members from the shame of the witch trials, Alexander changed his name from Hogg to the far more pious Church? (See Index in back of book). Additional evidence recently discovered indicates that our twenty-first president of the United States, Chester A. Arthur, is himself a direct descendant of Susannah Martin.

Maybe in the end we are all one, all brothers, faced with the unenviable challenge in our lives, of bringing people together rather than separating ourselves through factions, ideals, races, political affiliations, religions and prejudice.

Maybe through our divisions and lack of harmony, which are counterproductive to our acceptance of each other, we on earth are then ultimately responsible for our own demise.

The Salem witch trials were a dark, dark time in our Nation's history. Every one of us is a creature of our heavenly Father and everyone has redeeming qualities. However, it is not our right to judge: *Judge not and ye shall not be judged.* If we learn from the past, the future will be a bright one. Love is the answer, the antidote, the key. Yes, there is evil all around us, but we can temper such with love. We can see each day as an opportunity to love a little bit more. Love those you love. Love those you hate. It is when you truly start to love ALL, that the world improves. Strangers become friends, foes become allies. New partnerships sprout and grow. As we accept ourselves as one in genealogical flesh as we do in spirit, the world becomes a smaller neighborhood. We must realize that we are all ONE in the Father. The sooner we act as one, the sooner the world will change and there will be peace on earth.

Just as nature's spring leaves sprout, grow, mature, and turn vibrant, before succumbing to their annual demise, we too mirror this process. We do sprout again, as other colors, other shapes, other sizes, other genders, in other times. These successive springs and autumns let us grow closer to the Lord. The desire is for perfection in God's eyes. Is our ultimate goal, in fact, the evolution of our soul? If so, we must overcome our ego desires and work towards self-discovery in an imperfect world. As I have learned, we can do so only by trusting in others and releasing our fears. In this way we can thus attain our greatest spirituality.

This wonderful God-given cycle of life we experience here and now is that of nature, the same howling wilderness encountered by the Puritans. But what happens when the darker sides of this nature infiltrate the human community itself with a power of their own, contrary to God's love and perhaps His own will? The witch trials were such and committed an inconceivable persecution. They have left a great scar on the community and a feeling that can not only be felt by New England's residents themselves, but its visitors and the generations of souls that are forever linked to this occurrence. As a human race we must learn to respect each other and bring a sense of tolerance to a world so pitted against one another. We must all pray that mankind can find strength to overcome this mind set. If we can't, the Salem Witch Trials will forever be a symbol of humanity's intolerant past and most regrettably, its irreconcilable future.

Index

(Actual document from 1809)

An act altering the names of Alexander Hogg, John Hogg, and Samuel Hogg.

"Whereas, Alexander Hogg, John Hogg, and Samuel Hogg, all of Orange in the County of Orange, have petitioned the Legislature to alter their names to Alexander Church, John Church and Samuel Church, and that the surnames of their children be likewise altered to that of Church

Therefore,

If it is hereby enacted by the General Assembly of the State of Vermont That the names of the said Alexander Hogg, John Hogg and Samuel Hogg, and the surname of their children, be, and the same are hereby altered from that of Hogg to that of Church and that they shall hereafter be called & known by, the name of Church instead of Hogg.

Passed October 27, 1809